The Case of the Vanishing Fishhook

The Case of the
Vanishing Fishhook

John R. Erickson

Illustrations by Gerald L. Holmes

Viking

VIKING
Published by the Penguin Group
Penguin Putnam Books for Young Readers, 345 Hudson Street, New York, New
York 10014, U.S.A.
Penguin Books Ltd, 27 Wrights Lane, London W8 5TZ, England
Penguin Books Australia Ltd, Ringwood, Victoria, Australia
Penguin Books Canada Ltd, 10 Alcorn Avenue, Toronto, Ontario, Canada M4V
3B2
Penguin Books (N.Z.) Ltd, 182-190 Wairau Road, Auckland 10, New Zealand

Penguin Books Ltd, Registered Offices: Harmondsworth, Middlesex, England

Published simultaneously by Viking and Puffin Books, members of Penguin
Putnam Books for Young Readers, 1999

5 7 9 10 8 6 4

Viking ISBN 0-670-88438-3

Printed in the United States of America
Set in New Century Schoolbook

Another one for my wife, Kristine.

CONTENTS

The Case of the
Vanishing Fishhook

CHAPTER ONE

An Enemy Submarine Invades Our Ranch

It's me again, Hank the Cowdog. It all began one dark night in July, as I recall. Yes, it was July. We'd already had June, and July is the month that follows June, right? Anyhow, that's the way it usually works, so, yes, we were in the month of July.

I was sleeping on my gunnysack bed beneath the gas tanks, minding my own business and trying to recover from the grinding routine of running my ranch. If I'd had anything in particular on my mind, the last thing on my mind would have been fishing. Or swallowing a fishhook. Never in my wildest dreams would I have thought that I would ever swallow a fishhook or that I would have to be rushed to the . . .

Oops. I'm getting ahead of myself. Forget I said anything about a fishhook. Just skip it.

Where were we? Oh yes, exhausted and asleep under the gas tanks. Maybe you've heard the expression "dog-tired," as in the statement, "He was dog-tired."

Well, there's a reason why such an expression exists, and it has nothing to do with fishing or fishhooks. The reason is that a dog such as myself has to put in eighteen hours a day to keep the ranch going. At the end of one of those long days—and we're talking about days when the temperature climbs up to a hundred degrees or even higher—at the end of one of those scorching summer days, a guy staggers home at ten o'clock at night, falls into his gunnysack bed, and tries to grab a few winks of sleep, so he'll be ready to do it all over again come daylight.

To use the old expression, he's "dog-tired."

Yes, the work and worry, the cares and responsibilities of running my ranch had just about worn me down to a shadow of my former self, and there I was on the old gunnysack, trying to recover from all the exhaustion and so forth.

That's when I awoke and heard the sounds of

someone or something creeping around in the darkness. It must have been around five o'clock in the morning, quite a bit too early for anyone on our outfit to be creeping around.

Most of your ordinary ranch mutts would have ignored the sound and gone back to sleep. Not me. As you may know, I'm Head of Ranch Security. I'm also pretty serious about it. When someone is creeping around my ranch before daylight, I want to know who it is and who gave him permission to be out there in the dark.

I lifted my head and tried to coordinate the position of my ears so as to maximize their ability to gather in sounds and vibrations. It's pretty important that a dog get those ears pointed in the proper direction, see, otherwise he'll end up listening to nonsense signals that can throw him off the track of the trail.

Well, I went right to work—activated the Earatory Scanner Network and began "sweeping," as we call it, the entire Western Quadrant of headquarters. And suddenly I found myself picking up signals that . . . well, just didn't make much sense.

See, my left ear was beaming data saying that someone, perhaps a human person, was out there in the darkness. But my right ear was send-

3

ing a totally different report to Data Control. It said that we were *picking up an enemy submarine on radar.*

Pretty shocking, huh? You bet it was. I mean, those two reports were very different, yet both had been gathered by my very own ears. Something was wrong here.

A lot of your ordinary ranch mutts would have considered it a hopeless situation. They would have quit and gone back to sleep. Not me, fellers. One of those reports was phoney and I intended to run Diagnostics until I found the error.

I mean, if we had an enemy submarine running loose on the ranch, someone needed to know about it and start barking an alarm, right? I decided to check with my Assistant of the Watch to see if he'd been picking up any strange signals on his equipment.

"Drover, wake up. Report to the bridge at once."

"Bridge over troubled porkchops . . . lorkin murgle snork."

"We've got a problem. We're getting garbage reports on the Earatory Scanners."

"No thanks, I just ate, and there's too many potato peelings."

"Not potato peelings, Drover. We have reason to think it might be an enemy submarine."

4

His head came up. "Hank, is that you?"

I stared at the face in the darkness. "Affirmative. That is, I think so."

"Oh good. If you're Hank, then I must be Drover. What are we doing here?"

"I . . . I'm not sure. I was sound asleep when all at once we started getting reports about . . . an enemy submarine, I think."

"I'll be derned."

"How about you?"

"Oh, pretty good, thanks. I must have been asleep too."

"Hmm, yes. That makes both of us, doesn't it?"

"Yeah." He yawned. "I wonder what woke us up."

"I . . . I don't remember. Did you wake me up?"

"I don't think so. Seems like you woke me up."

"Hmm, that's odd. Why would I have awakened you in the middle of the night? It must have been something important, but I can't . . . Drover, I'm almost sure that you woke me up. What was the reason? Concentrate. Try to remember."

"Well, okay, let's see here."

There was a long moment of silence. "Drover, did you go back to sleep?"

"No, I'm thinking. I don't think too fast in the dark."

"I see. What does darkness have to do with your thought processes?"

"Well, when I can't see anything, it's hard to think. I guess. Does that make sense?"

"No. Your brain lives in the dark all the time. It's inside your head, don't you see, and the inside portion of your head is dark."

"I'll be derned. How did you know that?"

"Because you have no windows."

"What about my eyes?"

"They're brown."

"Thanks."

There was another long moment of silence. "Drover, I'm beginning to feel that our conversation lacks meaning and purpose. Why are we awake at this hour of the night, and why are we talking at all? We should both be asleep."

"Yeah, I think we were, but then we woke up."

"Right, and that brings us to the nut of the fruit. What woke us up?"

"I was trying to remember that, but then it was too dark. Let's see here."

"Wait, hold everything. I remember now. You woke me up and said something about . . . picking up an enemy submarine, I think."

"That sounds pretty crazy. With my teeth?"

"What?"

"I said, did I pick it up with my teeth?"

"Pick *what* up with your teeth?"

"The enemy submarine."

"What are you talking about?"

"Well, I don't know. You said I said I picked up an enemy submarine in my jaws and . . . did something with it."

"I did not say that. In the first place, submarines are very heavy. Number two, there isn't enough water on this ranch to support a submarine. And number three, none of our enemies own a submarine. Therefore, the weight of the evidence suggests that you are talking nonsense."

"Can I go back to bed?"

"Not just yet." I stood up and walked a few steps away. "Drover, I think I'm beginning to understand this deal."

"Oh good."

"You see, we were both in a deep sleep, then something woke us up. I think this bizarre conversation can be traced back to the fact that—" Suddenly, I whirled around and faced him. "Drover, up until this very moment, we've been half-asleep. That would account for your claim that you ate a submarine."

"Yeah, and maybe it was a submarine sandwich, not a real submarine."

"Now we're getting somewhere. That makes sense, doesn't it? You were dreaming about food."

"Yeah, I love food. I'd rather eat food than anything. And I am kind of hungry."

"See? There you are. Your sleeping mind transformed your hunger into a dream about a submarine sandwich. It all fits together. We were merely talking in our respective sleeps, Drover. It could have happened to any two dogs on the globe."

"If we live on a globe, how come we don't fall off?"

"Good question, son. Ask it again some time."
I hurried back to my gunnysack. "Good night.
Hold my calls and don't wake me up again."

"Nightie-night."

"Nightie . . . snork murgle muff womp."

"Hank? I just heard something down at the
corrals."

"Murf snirk puffing triangles."

"Hank, I think you'd better wake up. Someone's
down there, no fooling. I see a light in the saddle
shed."

I sat up, pried open my eyes, and rushed to
the radar screen of my mind. There, before my
very eyes, as plain as day, I saw . . .

I leaped to my feet. "Holy smokes, Drivel,
there's an enemy submarine down by the saddle
shed!"

"My name's Drover."

"Never mind your name. Battle stations! Red
Alert!"

"It was only a sandwich."

"This is no sandwich, Drover, and it's no drill.
This is the real stuff. Come on, son, we'd better go
in for a closer look."

And with that, we went streaking down to the
saddle shed to find out exactly what that submarine was doing on my ranch.

CHAPTER TWO

Okay, Maybe It Wasn't a Submarine

We need to get something straight right here. You remember that report of an enemy submarine on the ranch? It turned out to be incorrect. There was no submarine, just as I had suspected.

See, when we make rapid shifts from asleepness to awakeness, it sometimes causes interference patterns to develop in our, uh, instruments. We get false images on our Earatory Radar and sometimes . . .

It's too complicated to explain. It was an instrumentation problem, and once I had made the sprint down to the corrals, everything had cleared up and I began to realize that the business about the "enemy submarine" was bogus.

It wasn't an enemy submarine. It was Slim

Chance, the hired hand on this outfit. But what the heck was he doing down at the corrals in the middle of the night? At first I thought he might have been walking in his sleep. Then I remembered that his shack ... house ... the place where he stayed and slept at night was two miles down the creek, which made the Sleepwalking Hypotenuse highly unlikely.

Nobody walks two miles in his sleep. So I probed the matter deeper and in more detail until I came up with a solid explanation.

You know what he was doing? He'd gotten out of bed and had driven up to headquarters to check on a first-calf heifer that was about to deliver her first calf.

Have we discussed heifers and the process of calving them out? Maybe not. It's an important job and I happen to know quite a bit about it. Here's the deal. Every year the ranch has to replace old cows with young cows. Young cows are called "heifers," and if you want to know why, ask a heifer. I don't know.

What would be wrong with calling them "young cows"? That would be much simpler and then you wouldn't have to remember whether "heifer" is spelled "heifer" or "hiefer" or "heffer," but nobody asked my opinion.

Every year our ranch saves 20 or 30 heifers, and when the time comes for them to deliver their calves, Slim has to watch them closely, because sometimes heifers have trouble. If they don't get help from the local cowboy-vet, the calf might die, and sometimes the heffer... heiffer... sometimes the young cow will die too.

Slim has to check them in the middle of the night and sometimes he just sleeps down at the barn with them. If they have trouble shelling out the calf, he assists them.

He calls himself "Dr. Slim," but I think that's some kind of joke. I don't think he actually has a doctor's degree.

I'm sure he doesn't.

Anyways, I have watched him deliver calves on several occasions—I being his most trusted assistant and also the only one on the ranch who will stay up all night with him in a drafty shed— and I know the procedure fairly well.

It's called "pulling a calf" and it's done with two pieces of equipment: a small-gauge chain with a loop on each end (it's called an "O.B. chain") and a device called a "calf-puller." Shall we run through the procedure? Might as well.

Okay, here's the deal. When the heifer has been straining for several hours and hasn't

shelled out the calf, Dr. Slim throws his rope over
the heifer's horns and snubs her up to a post. The
reason for this is that young cow mothers don't
always appreciate having a cowboy doctor in the
pen with them and will sometimes try to run him
out of the operating room.

With the heifer tied to the snubbing post, Dr.

Slim loops the ends of the chain around the baby calf's front feet, then hooks the chain into the calf-puller, which has a cranking device that pulls the calf out. He ratchets the lever while the heifer strains, and after a minute or two the calf pops out and lands on the ground.

Pretty slick, huh? And it's pretty impressive that a dog would know so much about medical science, but knowing such things is just part of my job as Head of Ranch Security.

I had watched Slim pull dozens of calves, but this time I noticed that something was different. For one thing, the heifer was already lying on the ground when we got there, and Dr. Slim decided he wouldn't need to snub her to the post. Bad idea.

For another thing, Slim had left his calf-pullers up at the machine shed. Was that smart? No, it was unsmart and also very careless of him. If he had a pregnant heifer in the corrals, why had he left the calf-pullers in the machine shed? I have no idea, but I sure wouldn't have done it that way.

Anyways, the heifer was laid out on the ground and was trying to squeeze out her calf. Dr. Slim sized up the situation, chewed his lip for five seconds, and came up with a plan.

Here's what he said, word for word. He said, "Welp, she's down so I don't need to snub her, and I ain't got time to go chuggin' up to the machine shed for the calf-pullers, so we'll pull this little feller *the cowboy way*."

And then he gave me a wink. Why did he wink at me? I already knew that he'd just made the dumbest decision of the week and that this was going to turn into a train wreck. He should have saved his wink or given it to someone else who didn't know what was coming.

I heaved a sigh, rolled my eyes towards heaven, and waited for the ineffible to happen.

Uneffible.

Interebbible.

Do you have any idea what it means to pull a calf "the cowboy way?" It's a special technique cowboys use when they are out in the pasture with no calf-pulling equipment at hand, or when they're too lazy to gather up the proper equipment, or when their lives have gotten so dull that they need some excitement.

You guess which one applied to Slim.

Here's what he did. He looped one end of his O.B. chain around the calf's front feet and then he looped the other end of the chain *around his right wrist*.

Do you see what's coming? I did. I could have told him . . . in fact, I tried to tell him. I barked three times, hoping to bark some sense into his thick skull, but did he listen? Oh no. I was just a dumb dog and he was Mister Expert on Pulling Calves and Just About Everything Else, and so naturally he didn't listen to the Voice of Reason.

He sat down on the ground, braced his feet against the heifer's hips, and began tugging on the chain. Oh, and he said, "This won't take but a minute."

Ha.

If you were a young cow mother, lying on the ground and trying to deliver a calf, and some guy started pushing on your hips with his boots and pulling on you with a chain, would you just lie there and be sweet about it? I wouldn't have, and neither did that heifer.

One second she was lying on the ground, and the next second she was on her feet—snorting, bellering, blowing smoke, and throwing her horns.

Well, I saw the wreck coming and I knew that it was up to me to save Slim from his bonehead behavior. I sprang into action with a burst of barking, then dived in front of the heifer and bit her on the nose. At the time it seemed a good strategy. See, if she came after me, she couldn't possibly harm Dr. Bonehead with her horns, right?

But all at once Slim was squalling. "Hank, don't get her stirred up! Leave her alone!"

HUH?

Okay, I hadn't considered that once she began chasing me around the corral, Slim would be ... don't forget that he'd looped that chain around his wrist, and don't forget that I'd had nothing to do with that decision. I never would have done such a crazy thing.

Well, she came after me, sure enough, and let me tell you about heifers in labor. They're in a real bad mood to start with, and then you add one cowboy doctor and one barking dog and ...

She was real unhappy about the whole situation and she let me know right away that she had every intention of harming someone. What was I supposed to do, sit there and get myself run over by a train with horns? Forget that. I ran, fellers.

We made several laps around the corral. The good news was that I managed to stay a step ahead of her deadly horns and thus saved the ranch the price of a funeral. The bad news was that . . . well, old Slim was attached to her by a chain and as we lapped the corral, he sure moved a lot of dirt. And fresh manure. He looked like a propeller tied to the cow's tail, is how he looked.

It was on our third lap around the pen when he got wrapped around the snubbing post. That tightened the chain and, bingo, a cute little black baldface calf made his entrance into the world. The heifer must have noticed that something was different. She stopped, sniffed the air, bawled, and looked back towards her calf.

And Slim. He undid the chain, got up on his hands and knees, and let out a groan. Maybe the heifer thought she'd given birth to a cowboy instead of a calf. Anyways she went over and gave him a sniffing. He looked pretty strange, I must admit. He'd bulldozed so much dirt with his face that it had turned brown. Oh, and the back of his white shirt had a big green splotch on it, the exact color of recycled grass.

That snubbing post had knocked the wind out of him and he wasn't in the mood to be sniffed, I suppose. He waved a hat in front of her face and said, "Get out of here, you old bat." Another bad idea. The heifer decided that who-ever that guy was on the ground, he had no business lurking around her new calf. She dropped her head, shook her horns, bellered, and started pawing up dirt.

Slim got to his feet and made a run for it. The heifer followed and was taking aim at his back pockets when I decided to spring into action. I left my spot on the other side of the corral fence and went charging into battle. I think I could have saved him if he hadn't . . . well, gotten his feet tangled up on . . . well, on ME, you might say.

I don't know how it happened. Apparently Slim wasn't paying attention to his business. I think he could have missed me if he'd . . . okay, maybe I ran between his legs, but don't forget that it was very dark out there and I was just trying to help. And don't forget that I was concentrating on an insane heifer with horns.

"Hank, get out of the way!"

Anyways, Slim did another dive into the dirt and all at once I found myself positioned between him and the heifer. She stopped and we glared into each other's eyes. Her head was shaking. Her eyes were on fire and bulging out of her head. Smoke and steam and burning lava hissed out of her nostrils.

I was cornered, trapped, exposed, and all at once I realized that heroism had been thrust upon me. I decided to show her some fangs and address her in a firm term of voice: "Listen, you old hag, if you don't..."

Maybe we'd better not go on. The next part is so scary, I'm not sure I should reveal it. No kidding. You know how I am about the kids. I don't mind giving 'em a little thrill now and then, but the real hardcore, heavy-duty scary stuff...

Better skip it.

Sorry.

Caution:
Scary Material!

What? You think you can handle the scary part? Well, maybe you can and maybe you can't. I guess we can give it a try and see what happens, but if you end up having nightmares or wetting the bed, don't blame me.

I tried to warn you.

Okay, back to the enraged heifer. Yipes! It was pretty clear that she had no desire to work this thing out or come up with a peaceful solution. In one rapid motion, she scooped me up on her horns and tossed me into the air like a feather. When I came back to earth, she was right there, waiting to do it again. She did.

Hey, I could take a hint. If she didn't want me in her nursery, that was fine. I was ready to

leave, but it wasn't so easy to get out when I was spending so much of my time doing loops and cartwheels in the air.

The old hag . . . young hag. The hateful thing.

Well, it took some doing, but at last I was able to escape her horns and scramble under the fence to safety. There, I joined Slim who was bent over with his hands on his knees, trying to catch his breath. I sat down at his feet and swept the ground with my tail, as if to say, "Well, how'd we do?"

His eyes came up and pierced me. "You know, Hank, there's times when I think our friendship ain't worth all the trouble it causes. Next time I have to pull a calf, would you take a trip to the Belgium Congo and stay gone for a month?"

Well, I . . . I hardly knew how to respond to that. I mean, I'd tried to do my part.

The heifer had gone over to her calf and was licking it down, but every now and then her head jerked around and she gave us menacing glares. Slim raised up, rubbed his ribs, and let out a groan.

"Well, it's been a night for higher education, and I have learned an important lesson about pulling calves the Cowboy Way. Next time, I think I'll just foller the manual."

See? I'd tried to tell him.

He fished a pocket watch out of his jeans. He

snapped open the case and brought the watch up close to his face. He squinted and scowled. "Good honk, I'm going blind, can't even see the hands on this watch." He gave it a shake. It made a rattling sound. "Oh. I wondered what that crunch was when I wrapped around the snubbin' post. I thought it was my broken heart but I guess it was my watch."

He heaved a sigh and put his busted watch away. "I'm guessing it's about five o'clock in the A and M—too early to start work and too late to go back to the house. You reckon we might ought to drive into town and get some breakfast at the cafe?"

Drive 25 miles into town? In the dark? Not me, pal. I wasn't that desperate for something to eat.

He must have figured this out on his own. "Naw, too much trouble." He yawned and stretched. "Well, I'm going to make me a pallet on the saddle shed floor and catch a few winks. How about you, pup?"

Me? No, I still had rounds to make, things to . . . oh, what the heck, maybe the ranch could survive if I grabbed a few hours' sleep. Sure.

We groped our way to the saddle shed. Slim gathered up four saddle blankets and laid them out on the floor. Say, that looked pretty inviting, and

I moved right in and began scratching up my . . .

"Hey, don't be digging up my bed. You can sleep on the floor."

Well . . . sure, fine. I was just . . . gee, he was awfully grabby about the bed.

He snapped off the light and stretched out on my . . . on the bed, shall we say, while I sat on the hard cement floor.

"Ahhhh! Heck of a fine bed. Don't know as I've ever stretched out on a better bed. You'd love it, pooch, only we ain't got any room for you. Sorry."

That was okay. I knew his sleeping habits. We would experience thirty seconds of silence, then the air would be filled with his honking and snoring, and at that point I would, heh-heh, find my rightful place on the bed.

Sure enough, silence moved over us. I waited for my signal. Ten seconds. Fifteen seconds. Twenty seconds. Then . . .

"Hank, have I ever sung you the song about Billy Joe and Dave?"

What? The song about . . . hey, it was five o'clock in the morning!

"I'll bet you'd love to hear it."

No, I would NOT love to hear it. I would love to SLEEP. That's what most people did at this hour of the morning.

"I wouldn't sing for just any old mutt. I hope you know that."

Oh brother.

"You're a mighty lucky dog."

Yeah, right.

"I hope I can remember all the words. You'd forgive me if I messed up a verse or two, wouldn't you?"

Sigh. It appeared that I was about to be exposed to another one of his corny songs. A dog sure has to put up with a lot on this outfit.

Have we discussed Slim's singing? He wasn't much of a singer, but he didn't know it or wouldn't admit it. He came up with these corny songs and then performed them for *me*. Why me, out of all the people and dogs in the world? How could I be so lucky?

Because nobody else would sit there and listen to it. I had to. It was part of my job, and it wasn't the part I liked the best. I had to sit there and stay awake and pretend that I was listening to something wonderful.

I waited to hear the tiresome thing—his song, that is. I waited and waited. The next thing I heard was the sound of his snoring.

He was asleep!

What was the deal? After I'd gone to the trouble to prepare myself for the shock of his so-called music, he'd . . . oh well. It was no big loss.

I had dodged a bullet, but by then I was wide awerp and ready to launch mysnork into another eighteen-hour day of wonk. There was no womp I would be urble to snork the honking sassafras smurk skittlebum . . . zzzzzzzzz.

Okay, maybe I dozed off. Who wouldn't have dozed off? Don't forget, I had been up most of the night, protecting the ranch and calving out heifers. I was tuckered out and in desperate need of sleep, so I grabbed me a few Z's.

What woke me up was the sound of someone making an unauthorized entry into the . . . where was I? My head shot up and I managed to squeeze off a bark or two. Okay, I was in the saddle shed, and at first I aimed a bark at Slim because I thought . . . I don't know what I thought, but there was this guy stretched out on the floor and that seemed pretty strange.

But then the door opened and sunlight poured in, and through the glare of sunbeams I saw some kind of midget standing there in the doorway, so I turned my guns around and aimed several barks at . . .

Huh? Okay, it turned out to be Little Alfred. Relax. I canceled the Code Three and shifted into the Grins and Wags Procedure.

See, Slim and I had fallen asleep in the saddle shed, and ... maybe you remember that part, so let's move along. Slim sat up, yawned, and rubbed his eyes. Then he squinted at me and wrinkled up his nose and pushed me away.

"Hank, has anyone told you lately that you stink? Well, you do. I'd sooner sleep with hogs."

There, you see? I'd stayed up half the night with him, had saved him from being trampled and skewered by an angry heifer, and that was all the thanks I got for it. He hadn't cared about my smell when I'd been out there in the corral, saving his life, but now ...

Oh well. Putting up with his childish remarks was just part of the job, but I'll tell you something. *He didn't smell so great himself.* I mean, we're talking about a bachelor cowboy who spent very little time in a bathtub, right? And a guy who'd recently been dragged through a cow lot, right?

But did I make a big deal out of that? Did I go around telling everyone on the ranch that he smelled worse than hogs? No sir. All I did was ... oh well.

Sticks and stones may break my bones, but I didn't smell a bit worse than he did.

And if he didn't want me sitting close to him, that was just fine with me. I had other friends in the world, people who really cared about me and accepted me for what I was and didn't mind if I smelled a little . . . well, ranchy.

How's a ranch dog supposed to smell?

I jacked myself up off the floor, left Slim to enjoy his own boring company, and marched straight over to Little Alfred. And there, right in front of my former friend, I hopped up on my back legs and gave the boy a juicy lick on the cheek.

He laughed and gave me a hug. "Hi, Hankie. What are y'all doing down here in the saddo shed? Were you sweeping?"

Slim dragged himself up to a standing position, groaned, and rubbed his side. He explained that we had been calving out a heifer. "What time is it?"

"Oh, ten o'cwock, I guess."

"Good honk. The day's half over. I need to get some work done." He yawned. "I wish them heifers would have their children during my office hours. They sure get my days and nights messed up."

"Hey Swim, I've got a gweat idea. Why don't we pway Tom Sawyer and Huckleberry Finn? Me and my dad have been weading the book at night."

"The heck you have."

"Yep. I'll be Tom Sawyer. You can be Huck, and we'll go down to the Mississippi Wiver and catch fish."

Slim nodded his head and thought about it. "You know, Button, that sounds like a lot of fun, but I've got a handicap that keeps me from doing stuff like that. It's called a steady job."

"Aw, Swim."

"See, your daddy pays my wages and he wants me to play Slim Chance—cowboy vet, welder, hay-hauler, barn cleaner-upper, and windmill mechanic. He might not be tickled if I was to switch over to Huckleberry Finn."

The boy frowned and rocked up and down on his toes. "Well . . . he wikes the book. Maybe he wouldn't care."

"Heh. You don't know your daddy as well as I do, son. When it comes to ranch work, he's a regular Simon LaGreasy. I think I'd better pass on the Huck Finn offer."

Alfred's face fell into a heap of wrinkles and he pooched out his lips. "Dwat. I can't pway Tom Sawyer without a Huckleberry Finn."

Slim snapped his fingers. "I know just the guy for the Huck Finn part." All at once his gaze swung around and fastened on . . . well, on ME, you might say.

Hey, what was this all about? I soon found out, and that's where the Fishhook Deal came from.

CHAPTER FOUR

Attacked by a Huge One-Eyed Robot

They were staring at me, both of them, and grinning. What was the deal? I gave them Sincere Looks and whapped my tail on the cement floor, as if to say, "Sorry, I wasn't listening and must have missed part of the, uh, conversation."

I'd heard part of it. Alfred and his dad had been reading some book about a guy who went fishing and . . . ate strawberries . . . huckleberries . . . something about berries, and Slim had been offered a job . . .

To tell you the truth, it hadn't made much sense to me and . . . why were they grinning at me?

Alfred looked up at Slim. "You think Hank could be Huck?"

"Why shore, why not? 'Hank' is pretty close to 'Huck,' ain't it? I mean, you just shuffle a few letters around and you get Huck. And Huck, now, he was about half-lazy and worthless, as I remember, and that sort of fits too, don't it?"

Alfred thought that over. "Yeah, but in the book, Huck didn't have a tail."

"Huh. Hadn't thought of that. Say, we've got a hacksaw up at the machine shed, and I'll bet we could fix that tail business."

What? Fix my tail with a hacksaw, is that what he'd said? I searched their faces for some hint of what was going on here and . . . okay, they both laughed, so it appeared that this was some more of Slim's cowboy humor.

Around here, you never know for sure. I mean, just when you think he's kidding, you find out that it's a nutty idea and he's serious about it.

But this time he was kidding. I was glad.

Slim got his chuckle out of it and continued. "Heck, it don't matter that he has a tail. It's all pretend anyway. Now." He hitched up his jeans. "If y'all will excuse me, I need to start my day and get some work done. Some of us have to work for a living, you know."

Why did he glance at me when he said that? It was a cheap shot, another lame attempt at humor.

He thinks he's such a comedian. Sometimes . . . just skip it.

Alfred and I followed him outside. He closed the saddle shed door, then opened a corral gate so that the heifer and her new calf could go out into the pasture. Then the three of us hiked up the hill to the machine shed. Slim stopped in front of the shed and gave us a stern glare.

"Now listen, you two. I've got to do some welding to stay ahead of all the hay equipment your daddy tears up in a normal day. When I get under that welding hood and start burnin' sticks, y'all don't look at the fire, hear? It'll blister your eyes."

Alfred nodded. "Okay, Swim."

"And don't be getting into any mischief."

"Okay, Swim. We'll be so good, you'll think we're angels from heaven."

Slim's gaze went from me to Alfred and back to me. He shook his head. "Huh. Somehow I ain't convinced, but I guess we can give it a try."

He pushed open the big sliding doors and we all went inside. Slim gathered up some tools and equipment, and turned on the welder whilst Alfred and I found places to sit nearby. Just for a moment or two I was distracted by a flea on my right hind leg, and when I looked up again I saw . . .

HUH?

You won't believe this. *Slim had vanished,* and in his place there stood this . . . this . . . this HUGE ONE-EYED ROBOT. Honest. I'm not kidding. And it had the scariest face you ever saw—no ears, no nose, no wrinkles or expression, and one big eye in the shape of a box or a rectangle. It stretched across the upper part of his face, the eye did, and it was very dark, almost black.

Scariest thing I'd ever seen.

Well, you know me. When I'm confronted by

robots and monsters, I don't just sit there looking simple. I bark. Yes sir, and that's just what I did. I leaped to my feet, bristled the hair on my back, and launched myself into a withering barrage of barking.

Oh, and did I mention the ray gun in his right hand? Yes sir, he held some kind of deadly ray gun in his hand, and it was attached to a long black cord.

I didn't know who that guy was or what he was doing on our ranch, but I took no chances. I gave him the Full Load of barking, and also began edging towards the door. I had never gone up against a robot as big as this one. I'll bet he stood six feet tall.

Seven feet. The biggest, scariest robot I'd ever seen.

Well, I barked at him for a whole minute, I mean, one bark right after another, and it should have scared him away. But it didn't. You know what he did?

Hang on. This gets real scary.

He turned around very slowly and stared at me with that . . . that wicked black eye. The barking died in my throat. I froze and felt the hair rising on the back of my neck. Then . . .

Are you sure you ought to hear the rest of

this? Don't even try it unless you've had some experience with robots and monsters.

Okay, there we were. He was staring at me with his horrible robot eye and I was frozen in my tracks, waiting to see what would happen next. What happened next was that he raised his hands up to the level of his head, made claws with them, and *started slouching towards me.*

Oh, and he growled too, a deep ferocious growl.

Hey, that was all I needed to know about robots. THEY ATE DOGS!

I went to Full Power on all engines, spun all four paws on the cement floor, and got the heck out of there. Once I had cleared the door, I dared to fire a bark over my shoulder, just in case he might be . . .

Where was Little Alfred? I screeched to a stop. Holy smokes, the boy was trapped inside the machine shed with that bloodthirsty . . .

Huh? Laughter? I cocked my ears and listened. Unless I was badly mistaken, someone inside the machine shed . . . several someones inside the machine shed were . . . laughing. That made no sense. I mean, this was a very serious deal, so why would . . .

Did I dare creep back to the door and peek inside? It would be dangerous, but I had to do it. I

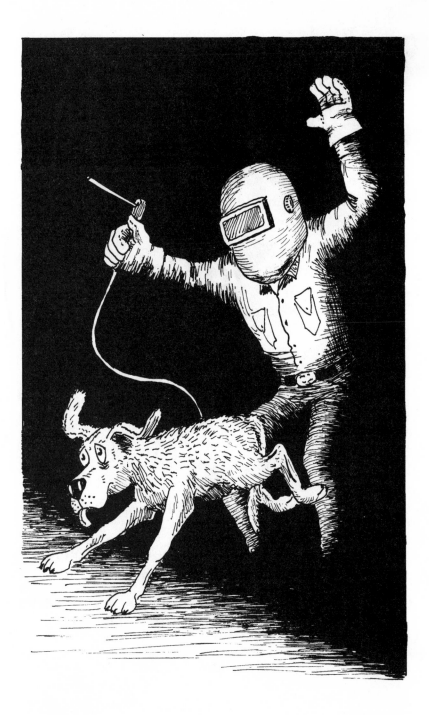

had to check on the boy. For all I knew, that robot monster had tied him up and was now . . . well, tickling him or something. That would account for his laughter, see.

Yes, I had to know the awful truth, so I forced myself to creep back to the door. My entire body was as tense as a coiled spring, the enormous muscles in my shoulders drawn as tight as bands of steel. Closer and closer I crept. I poked my head through the doors and saw . . .

Okay, false alarm, relax. It was another of Slim's stupid . . .

He was welding, right? And you probably didn't know that when people weld, they wear a black plastic hood, called a . . . well, a welding hood, of course. It has a slit of smoked glass that looks very much like a monster eye, see, and any dog who had seen . . .

Oh, he got big yuks out of this. He flipped up the hood and pointed to his face and said, "It's only me, you dufus dog."

Hey, I'd known it was him all along. He hadn't fooled . . .

He thinks he's so funny, but he's not, not funny at all. I don't know why I put up with his . . .

Skip it.

Holding my head at a proud angle, I marched

back into this so-called "workplace," which had been transformed into the scene of Slim's childish follyrot. I went straight over to my pal Alfred and gave him Looks of Embarrassment and Slow Wags on the tail section. It saddened me to see that he too was laughing.

"Did you think he was a monstoo, Hankie?"

No. Well, not for long. Could we move along to something else?

At last Slim's laughter faded away and he ran out of excuses to loaf and torment innocent dogs. At that point he lowered his welding hood and was forced to go to work. I know it must have broken his heart.

He's such a goof-off. And can you believe he'd called ME a "dufus dog"? Ha.

All at once the air was filled with sparks and smoke and the crackle of burning metal. Alfred and I sat there for a long time, concentrating extra hard on being perfect children and dogs. It turned out to be pretty boring, actually, and after ten minutes of it, the boy got up and started prowling around.

He played with some tools for a while, then he spied the ground clamp on the piece of metal Slim was welding. Welding on. The piece of metal on which he was . . . phooey.

39

There's this thing called a "ground lead." It's a thick black wire with a clamp on the end. When guys weld, they have to clamp the clamp on the piece of metal they're welding. Why? I have no idea, but I know that if you unhook the clamp, the welder quits working.

And that's what Alfred did. He unhooked the clamp and hooked it up to a pipe wrench that was lying on the floor. And all at once, the air was no longer filled with smoke and sparks and the crackle of burning metal. The welder quit.

In the silence we heard Slim scratching the welding rod over the piece of metal. The scratching grew louder and more vigorous. Then he leaped up and raised the hood.

"This dadgum two-bit crackerbox piece of junk! I told Loper to buy us a decent welder. How can I fix all the stuff he tears up when he won't . . ." The rest of what he said was lost in a fog of mumbles and mutters.

He stomped over to the welder and flicked the switch off and on several times. He leaned down and listened to the hum. He twisted several dials. Then he kicked it.

"Pig nose. Probably got a short. A mouse probably chewed a . . ." It was then that his eyes fell upon the ground lead, which was clamped to the

Stilson wrench. His gaze moved slowly across the room and landed on Alfred, like a cat pouncing on a mouse. "Did you do that?"

The boy was looking up at the ceiling. "Do what, Swim?"

"Uh-huh. I think it's time for y'all to move along."

"I was twying to help, Swim."

Slim took the boy by the ear and led him to the door. "Trying and helping ain't the same, son, and an idle mind is the devil's workshop."

"Aw, Swim, what'll we do?"

"Go play Tom Sawyer. Go get the mail. Go dig a hole. But the main thing is GO."

"What about my dog?"

"Let not your heart be troubled, he's next on the list to leave." Slim came back into the shop. He drilled me with a hot glare and jerked his thumb over his shoulder. "All right, bozo, the fun part's over. Scram."

Fine. I'd been about ready to leave anyway. Too much noise and smoke.

I gathered myself up, made a wide path around Slim the Robot, and plunged outside into the fresh air and sunshine.

Little did I know or suspect what lay ahead. It wasn't good.

CHAPTER FIVE

Little Alfred
Schemes Up a
Fishing Expedition

Once outside, I joined up with Little Alfred. For a while we sat in front of the machine shed, watching the chickens peck for grasshoppers and tossing rocks. Alfred tossed most of the rocks and I watched the chickens, if you want to get technical about it.

The morning air was starting to heat up and we began to wilt in the glare of the sun. The minutes dragged by. At last Little Alfred spoke.

"I'm bored. How about you, Hankie?"

Well, I hadn't thought much about it, but yes, now that he'd mentioned it, things did seem a little boring. I mean, when a guy finds himself watching chickens for sport, it's a pretty slow day. Yes, I too was bored.

He chuncked a rock at a hen, causing her to squawk and jump into the air. That brought a smile to his mouth, but it faded quickly. He heaved a sigh.

"I wonder what Tom Sawyer did when he got bored."

Well, I didn't know about that, seeing as how I'd never met Tom Sawyer and didn't know who he was. Wait a minute. Was he the guy in the book? Okay, he was some character in a book, but I hadn't read the book and didn't have an opinion.

"I think . . . he'd go fishing . . . in the Mississippi Wiver . . . with his best pal, Huckleberry Finn."

Hmm. Maybe so.

A little gleam had come into his eyes. "Wet's go fishing, Hankie, just you and me. I'll get my pole and tackle box out of my woom, and I'll get some beef liver for bait, and we'll go down to the Mississippi Wiver and catch some big old fish."

Hmm. Well, that did sound kind of exciting.

He was on his feet now, walking towards the house. "I'll be Tom Sawyer and you can be Huck Finn. Won't that be fun?"

Well, I . . . maybe so. I mean, I had never played

this game before and I didn't know exactly what was required of a dog to be Huck Finn, but what the heck, I was open to new experiences and adventures. Sure.

The farther we walked down the hill, the more excited we both became about the fishing expedition. It was sounding better all the time. But when we reached the bottom of the hill, a shadow passed over the boy's face. He stopped, and his gaze went straight to . . .

I followed his gaze and saw . . . uh oh . . . Sally May, his mom, was working in a flower bed near the yard gate. Have we discussed Sally May? Maybe not.

Let me begin by saying that she was a fine lady and a wonderful mother, but there was something about her that . . . how can I put this? There was something about her that, uh, struck fear in the hearts of dogs and little boys.

Well, maybe it wasn't exactly fear. Call it *guilt*. See, it's a well known fact that dogs and little boys often have things on their minds which might not, uh, meet the approval of the Lady of the House. And the scary thing about Sally May was that *she always seemed to know.*

She could read faces. She could read minds. She never slept. She saw everything and knew everything. She had eyes in the back of her head and ears that could hear ants crawling in the next pasture, and her nose . . . you couldn't sneak anything past that nose of hers. She had a nose like a bloodhound.

And every time I came into her presence, I began to . . . wilt. And fidget. I found it hard to look her in the eyes and I began to experience powerful feelings of guilt—even when I hadn't done anything wrong. And sometimes I even got the feeling that . . . well, that she just didn't like me.

That's hard to believe, isn't it? Maybe it was my imagination, but I sure got that feeling.

Anyhow, there she was beside the yard gate, and her very presence stopped us in our tracks. Alfred dropped his voice to a whisper.

"Mom might not wet me go fishing, so we'll have to be sneaky."

I whapped my tail on the ground and stared at him. Be sneaky? Around Sally May? Was he serious? Ha! Trying to sneak something past his mother was like holding a skunk under a bloodhound's nose and saying, "Do you smell anything?" It wouldn't work.

The boy ignored me. "I'll sneak into the house and get my stuff. You visit with my mom and keep her busy, and I'll sneak out the fwont door."

He gave me a wink and a smile. "She'll nevoo suspect a thing."

Oh yeah, right. She'd never suspect a thing.

Okay, I'd go along with this crazy plan, but I already knew where it was heading.

The boy arranged his face into an innocent expression, shoved his hands into the pockets of his overalls, and started walking towards the house. Oh, and he was whistling.

He walked through the gate and past Sally May. "Hi, Mom." He kept going.

Her head came up and she studied him with narrowed eyes. "Alfred, where are you going?"

"Oh, nowhere."

"Alfred."

"Into the house, Mom."

"For what?"

"Oh, I need a dwink."

She frowned and suddenly her gaze swung around to me. I felt as though someone had turned on a pair of searchlights, exposing me to all the world. Or stuck me with a fork. I found it hard to, uh, meet her gaze, and my eyes began wandering, so to speak, to the far horizon.

"Alfred, wipe your feet. I don't want you tracking barnyard into the house."

"Okay, Mom."

"And be very quiet. Molly's asleep."

"Okay, Mom."

"And don't snack. I'm fixing you a good nourishing lunch."

"Okay, Mom."

The boy disappeared inside the house. Her gaze lingered on the door and I could see Lines of Suspicion gathering on her brow. Well, it was time for me to swing into action with Diversionary Tactics—to use my charm, in other words, to take her mind off of Alfred's presence in the house.

To do this, I was forced to take bold action. I had to move through the gate and take several steps inside her yard—which happened to be Forbidden Territory to us dogs. Squeezing up my most charming and sincere smile, I edged through the gate and across the invisible line that separated the yard from the rest of the world. There, I waited to be recognized and greeted.

Oh, and I forgot to mention that for this mission, I switched my tail over to Slow Sensitive Wags. See, I knew she'd never go for Broad Swings or Joyful Wags. Those settings were a little too active and rough for a lady such as herself. If a guy wasn't paying attention to his business, he could sure get into trouble with those Broad Swings.

See, the womenfolk don't appreciate being whapped by a dog's tail, and sometimes your Broad Swings can damage flowers and stuff. Clearly, this was an occasion for Slow Sensitive Wags.

So there I stood beside her, a loyal dog waiting to be recognized, greeted, spoken to, and perhaps even petted and rubbed. A dog can always hope.

But she didn't notice me. Her eyes were still rivveted . . . rivitted . . . rivvitted . . . her eyes were still glued, shall we say, on the back door, through which Little Alfred had just passed. I waited patiently, but she continued to beam that suspicious eye towards the house.

I needed to get her attention, so I pulled up a program which I hadn't used in a long time. It was called "Here I Am," and it involved the use of a low whimper. As you might guess, I'm not the kind of dog who makes a habit of whimpering. Drover does it a lot, but I've never cared for it. But on this occasion, it seemed to fit.

So I ran "Here I Am" and gave her a whimper, with just a dash of quiver in the middle of it, and by George, it worked. It pulled her gaze away from the house, and all at once our faces were very close to each other and she was star-ing at me.

"Yes?"

That's all she said, and I must admit that a quick scan of her facial expression and so forth indicated that she was less than . . . well, over-joyed by my appearance, but what the heck, she had spoken to me and that was a start.

On a hunch, I cranked up the tail to Broader but Still Sensitive Wags. The message here was "Why, good morning, Sally May, and isn't it a beautiful day?"

"You're in my yard."

Oops. I switched back to Slow and Sensitive, and increased the sincerity of my smile. The mes-sage here was, "Yes, but I saw you working all alone, and I just couldn't resist coming over to, uh, share a few moments of . . . well, friendship and togetherness and so forth. No kidding."

I held my breath and waited for her response. Hey, it worked! I was really surprised. She reached out her soft white hand and began rubbing me behind the left ear.

"Okay, Hank. I'll give you a little sugar."

Wow, you talk about sugar. Those were some great rubs and scratches. My eyelids sagged to the half-open position, and I almost melted under the touch of her lovely hand.

Do you realize what a triumph this was? See, Sally May and I had ... that is, our relationship had suffered more than its share of ups and downs. We had gone through hardships and misunderstandings, yet here she was, scratching me behind the ears. And we were sharing a moment of real quality time—sharing the morning air, sharing our love of flowers and shrubberies and stuff, and sharing ... well, Life and the world and everything.

And even better, heh heh, she wasn't watching the house anymore, which was sort of the idea from the start. Another minute or two and my little pal would make his escape.

Oops. Just then she stopped scratching me and cocked her ear towards the house. I had to make a rapid response. I switched the tail section over to Circular Wags (those are pretty difficult) and toe-walked a little closer to her warm side. When she turned back to me, I was ready with Adoring Eyes and a smile of Extra Sincerity. This deal was really working and ...

Huh?

She stood up, dusted off her hands and jeans, and pushed me out the gate. "That's it. You can leave now." She closed the gate behind me.

Yeah but . . . gee, there for a minute I'd thought our relationship had . . . we'd shared so much and the emotions had . . .

She placed her hands on her hips and gave me an odd smile. "Do you think I don't know what you scamps are up to?"

Well, I . . .

She didn't even wait for my answer. She went striding through the yard, around the south side of the house, and captured Little Alfred just as he was sneaking out the door with his fishing pole and tackle box.

See? I told you. That woman knows everything. Nobody's safe around her.

Our mission had failed.

CHAPTER SIX

Pete Gets
Drenched, Tee-hee

Our mission had failed, but the most tragic part of it was that Sally May had almost broken my heart. I mean, there for a while I'd thought we had patched things up, formed a new relationship, reached a new platoon of emotional emotions, started all over again.

But then she'd dashed it all by shoving me out of the yard and saying, "That's it." All at once I felt used, tricked. I had dared to reveal tender emotions to this lady, had crawled out of my shell of . . . something.

Oh well. I hadn't expected it to work anyway. I mean, Sally May was a hard case. We dogs were pretty successful at fooling Slim and Loper, but Sally May was always tough. We could fool her once in a while, but not very often.

So, in spite of my broken heart and so forth, I wasn't exactly shocked when our plan fell as flat as a gutted snowbird and Little Alfred got captured going out the front door. I was still sitting beside the yard gate when his momma escorted him around to the backyard.

"No, Alfred Leroy, you may NOT go fishing by yourself."

"But Mom, I wasn't going awone. I was going wiff Hank."

A chirp of laughter shot out of her mouth. "Hank! Am I suppose to feel better about that? Sending you down to the creek with that dog?"

"He's a good dog, Mom."

"I know you think so, but to any mother in this world, sending you and Hank off to fish is like sending off Laurel to supervise Hardy. No."

"Aw Mom, pweese?"

"No. And if you want to argue about it, we'll go over to the hay field and discuss it with your father."

"But Mom, I'm bored. There's nothing to do awound here."

She stopped. Her brows rose and a smile spread across her mouth. "Oh really? Well, young man, I have just the cure for that." She seized his fishing pole and tackle box and set them down near the corner of the house. "You see these flowers and shrubs in the backyard? They all need to be watered."

The boy scowled and pooched out his lower lip. "That's not what I wanted to do."

"I'm sure it's not, but I have to go fix lunch for the men, and since you're so bored and can't think of anything to do, you can just do my watering."

His lip pooched out even further. "I don't even wike your dumb old fwowers."

She stiffened. "Do we need to talk to your father?" Alfred shook his head. "All right. Straighten up your attitude. The spray nozzle is on the hose. Give everything a good watering—*and don't make a mess.*"

"Bummer."

She towered over him and crossed her arms. "The proper response, young man, is not 'Bummer.' It's 'Yes, ma'am.' Now, try it again."

"Yes, ma'am."

"That's better. I'll be out to check on you when I get the potatoes whipped."

She went into the house. Alfred followed her with a dark scowl. Kicking at tuffs of grass, he sludged over to where I was sitting beside the gate.

"I got caught."

Yes, I'd noticed. And I'd be the last dog in the world to say, "I told you so."

"I have to water my mom's swubs. Tom Sawyer never had to water dumb old swubs."

Life was sometimes cruel.

"You want to come into the yard and help, Hankie?"

Uh . . . no thanks. I had gained a little ground with his mom and I wanted to hang onto it for a while. I would watch—and supervise—outside the yard.

He heaved a sigh, trudged over to the hydrant, and turned on the water. He picked up the hose and began watering the shrubberies. There was a spray attachment on the end of it, see, and he could change the shape and intensity of the spray by squeezing the handle.

I watched as he experimented with the thing, going from a broad mist to a single stream that squirted quite a long distance. It was fairly obvious that the best setting for this job was the broad mist, but it was just as obvious that the boy preferred the Fire Hose setting, with which he could send out a stream of water halfway across the yard.

This began to cause me some concern. Alfred

and I had been through a lot together, and I knew him pretty well. One of the things I knew about him was that he had a weakness for ornery tricks, and that he wouldn't be content watering plants for long.

There is a Universal Law of Physics which states ... let's see if I can remember the exact wording ... which states, "Loaded water hoses in the hands of little boys tend to go off in all directions." Yes, that's it, and as you might imagine, this began to cause me some concern.

See, even though Alfred and I were great pals, it was only a matter of time until he got bored with watering plants and began looking around for ... well, live targets, shall we say. And I had reason to suspect that he might include ME in that category.

I had just about made the decision to abandon my position at the gate and move my freight to a safer location, when suddenly and all at once something wonderful happened. In the course of spraying the shrubberies and flower beds, Alfred sent a shower of drops into the iris patch at the northeast corner of the house.

Would you care to guess who or whom was loafing in the iris patch, and who or whom got nailed by the spray? Tee-hee. Pete the Barncat. Mister

Never-Sweat. Mister Kitty Moocher. Mister Lurk-in-the-Flower-Beds.

Ho-ho, hee-hee, ha-ha.

Pete hated water. My ears shot up, my eyes popped open, and new meaning surged into the dusty corners of my life. All of a sudden I forgot the cares and responsibilities of running my ranch, and I prepared to indulge myself in the sheer delight of watching Kitty-Kitty get the hosing he so richly deserved.

Pete came flying out of the iris patch. His ears lay flat on his head and he wore a most unhappy expression on his face. Tee-hee. I could hardly contain myself. Ten feet west of the iris patch, he stopped and looked around. Then he began licking the water off his left hind leg.

Well, I was really involved now. Do you see the meaning of this? That cat was so dumb, he didn't know where the water had come from! No kidding. He didn't get it. I mean, there was a five-year-old ranch boy holding a loaded garden hose, and Pete thought the water had come from a passing cloud!

Hard to believe, huh? Not for those of us who study cats in great deeth and dovetail . . . great depth and detail, I should say. See, cats have a tiny form of intelligence. They're good at scheming and avoiding all forms of work, but they don't understand kids or cowboys. Your average ranch dog, on the other hand, will put the clues together (little boy + garden hose + shower of water) and figure it out in the brink of an eye.

How do we do it? Well, tremendous intellectual powers, for one thing, and also we understand the minds of ranch lads and cowboys.

But Pete missed it, totally missed it. He sat down in the grass to lick himself dry . . . and what do you suppose happened next? Heh-heh. You know. I know. Even Drover would have known. It was obvious to everyone on the ranch but Pete, and much to my joy and delight, he never saw it coming. And he got *fire-hosed*.

We're not talking about a little sprinkle, fellers, or a few stray drops that hit the mark. By this time, Little Alfred had mastered his weapon and had learned how to deliver the maximum amount of water to a small target. Pete got blasted, plastered, smeared.

I couldn't hold it back any longer. I laughed, I chortled, I guffawed, I snickered. I whooped for joy, barked, and moved my front paws up and down. Pete heard me and came at a run.

Seeing him in this soggy condition brought even more and deeper meaning into my life. I mean, the little snot was soaked to the bone. His whiskers were stuck together. His ears were pinned down and dribbling water. His hair was plastered into lumps, and his tail had lost all its fluff and now resembled the tail of a possum.

Tee-hee, ho-ho, ha-ha. It was wonderful.

He came slithering up and gave me an evil eye. "Well, Hankie, I guess you're enjoying this."

"You could say that, Kitty, yes. And it serves you right for being all the things you are: hateful, spiteful, sneaky, and greedy, just to name a few. Oh, and lazy. If you'd been out catching mice instead of loafing in the shade, this wouldn't have happened. You got exactly what you deserved, Kitty, and yes, I must admit..."

HUH?

Splat! Slosh! Slurp!

All at once my lecture was interrupted by a, uh, fire-hose torrent of water which... surely the boy had been aiming at the cat. I mean, we were pals, right, and we'd both been sharing the joy of seeing Pete's chickens come home to root... rot... roost... whatever...

We'd been sharing a precious moment of joy and happiness, and we were pals and we understood one another and... yikes, the little snipe was giggling and dragging the hose and running

in my direction . . . and there was a devilish gleam
in his eyes and . . .

SPLAT!

Forget what I said about him aiming at Pete.
He'd been aiming at ME, and this was no accident. He'd fire-hosed his best friend in the whole
world. I was shocked, outraged, wounded, and to
register my sense of wounded . . . SPLAT!

Okay, that did it. I should have known he'd . . .
I went to Full Throttle on all engines and got the
heck out of there. I ran into a patch of tall weeds
some fifteen yards west of the gate, and there I
stopped to repair the damage and check out the
situation.

The good news was that he'd run out of hose
and I was out of range of his stupid water. The
bad news was that he had managed to give me a
thorough soaking. The badder news was that
Pete and I were sharing the same patch of weeds.

He batted his eyelids and gave me his usual
smirking grin. "Now, what were you saying,
Hankie?"

I gave him a withering glare. "I was saying . . .
shut up, cat, and that's my last word on the
subject."

Well, Little Alfred had a big time squirting all
his friends on the ranch, but he should have
stopped there. He didn't, and when he saw his
mother's face at the kitchen window . . .

You'll never guess what he did.

CHAPTER SEVEN

Alfred Gets
in Big Trouble

I don't think he meant to cause as much trouble as he ended up causing. I figure it was just a passing impulse that seized him. He should have resisted it. Even I knew that. But he didn't.

There he was in the yard, see, with a loaded garden hose in his hands. He had scattered all the cats and dogs, and had become the King of the Yard. That's when he spied his mother. She was working at the kitchen sink, her face framed by the open window.

My guess is that a wicked thought popped into his head: Wouldn't it be funny if the hose somehow pointed itself towards the window screen and his mom somehow got sprayed?

I saw it coming but was helpless to do anything about it. It happened in a flash. With a flick of his wrist, he beamed a jet of water at the side of the house and began moving it southward, towards the open window. When it hit the window, we heard a screech from inside the house, and Sally May's face disappeared.

Well, he had wanted to get his mommy's attention, and he had certainly gotten it.

Moments later, she came boiling out the back door, throwing it open with such vigor that it hit the side of the house with a loud *whack*. Her face was red and something bad had happened to her hairdo. A prairie fire burned inside her eyeballs.

I was sitting in the weeds, some seventy-five feet west of the scene, yet the very sight of her caused me to melt into my tracks. It was clear, even at a distance, that Sally May had entered into one of her Thermonuclear Moments.

Birds stopped singing. Crickets ceased chirping. The wind stopped blowing. Ants scurried into their holes. Grasshoppers dived for cover. Butterflies sped away as fast as they could fly.

In that moment of awful silence, Little Alfred realized that he had made a BIG mistake, squirting his momma with the garden hose. He threw down the hose and headed for the front yard, pumping his little legs as fast as they would go.

"I didn't mean to, Mom. Honest. It was an accident."

"Alfred Leroy, you come back here!"

She started after him in a stiff-legged walk, swinging her arms. I had seen that walk before, and it sent chills of fear rolling down my backbone. I sank deeper into the weeds. She stalked around the side of the house and called his name again. He didn't answer. It appeared that he had gone into hiding.

Just then, Loper arrived for lunch. He stepped out of the pickup, slapped some hay dust off his clothes, and started towards the house. Sally May met him at the front gate and they held a high-level conference. I was far enough away so that I couldn't hear every word, but I heard enough to catch the drift of it.

"Your son . . . NOT funny . . . disrespectful . . . acting like a brat . . ."

Loper listened, nodded his head, and patted her on the arm. "I'll take care of it, hon."

"My hair is a mess. The little donkey."

Loper chuckled. "He's reminding me more and more of your side of the family."

At last a quick smile dashed across her mouth. "He's just like his daddy and you know it. Well, I left some peas on the stove. Lunch is ready."

She went back into the house. Then and only then did I dare come out of the weeds and slip down to the yard gate. I wanted to, uh, stay abreast of the latest breaking news, so to speak.

It didn't take Daddy long to flush Alfred out from the cedar shrub in front of the house. A couple of calls in that deep voice brought him out. With his head down, Alfred followed his dad around to the back of the house. There, they sat down on the step. Loper pushed his hat to the back of his head, placed his hands on Alfred's shoulders, and looked him in the eyes.

"I hear you squirted your mom with the hose."

The boy's head bobbed up and down.

"How did that happen?"

Alfred shrugged.

"Was it fun?"

That caught him by surprise. A grin leaped across his mouth and he nodded his head. "Yeah, but I didn't know she'd get so mad."

"Well, now you know. What you did was wrong. It was disrespectful. You chose to do it, you had your fun, and now you need to accept the consequences. I want you to take off your muddy boots, go into the house, and tell your mother you're sorry." Alfred nodded. "After lunch, you'll go to your room and stay there for two hours."

"Aw, Dad!"

"I want you to think about this. Are you listening? Never squirt your mother with the garden hose."

"Yeah, but I didn't mean . . ."

"Never squirt your mother with the garden hose. Understood?" The boy nodded. Loper offered his hand. "Shake on it. Now, take care of your business and let's put this behind us."

"Okay, Dad, but two whole hours?"

"Two whole hours. That's the price for your fun. Next time the price will be quite a bit higher—only there better not be a next time."

The boy shuffled off to the house, leading with a Big Lip. Just as he went inside, Slim came up from the machine shed for lunch. He sat down on the porch and began pulling off his boots. "What's wrong with Button? He's liable to step on that lip."

"Oh, he just got sentenced to two hours in solitary. Squirted his ma with the water hose."

Slim tried to hide his grin. "Mercy. Imagine, a son of yours doing such a thing."

"That's what my wife said, but I think it comes from him hanging around with you and that dog."

Huh? What dog? Surely he didn't . . . hey, I'd

just been sitting there, minding my own business and . . .

Oh well. They went inside for lunch, chuckling over their stale jokes. I didn't see the humor of it myself. I mean, I get into enough trouble around here without being blamed for Little Alfred's crimes.

And just for the record, let me state that I never would have sprayed Sally May with the garden hose. I've been accused of pulling a few dumb stunts, but never one as dumb as that.

Although it was kind of funny.

Well, there I was with nothing much to do and nobody to play with, now that my pal had been sent to jail. *Two whole hours!* It might as well have been two years.

Maybe you think I should have gone back to work—you know, made a patrol, barked at the mail truck, checked traffic on the county road, stuff like that—but it was already too derned hot. A guy needs to start those jobs earlier in the day. And besides, there was the matter of being a Loyal Dog.

See, when our pals get sent to jail, we dogs are sort of obligated to stick around to show Solidarity. How would it have looked if I had walked off and left him in there all alone? Not good. No, Showing Solidarity was part of the job and I had to do it, even though I hate sitting around and waiting.

It was boring, very boring. The minutes dragged by. I tried to amuse myself with the usual stuff. I gnawed at a couple of fleas, dug a hole, watched the clouds. Ho-hum. Slim and Loper came outside, rubbing their bellies and bragging about all the rhubarb pie they had eaten. (Nobody offered me any of that pie, by the way.) Then they parted company and went back to work.

After that little flurry of excitement, I settled back into the dull routine of snorking the borking rumpus . . . merf snerk . . . whiffen poof . . . I must have dozed off. Yes, I'm almost sure I did, and the next thing I knew, my eyes slid open and I saw . . .

Someone. A person. A small personish someone standing over me, with a fishing rod in one hand and a suitcase in the other. Wait, it wasn't a suitcase. It was too small to be a suitcase, so maybe . . . a tackle box?

Okay, while I had been dozing, this unidentified stranger had slipped into ranch headquarters and appeared to have some crazy ideas about fishing on my ranch, only we didn't allow unauthorized fishing, so I came roaring out of a deep sleep and . . .

Huh?

Okay, as my eyes adjusted to the darkness ... to the bright daylight, I should say ... once my eyes adjusted to the environmental situation that confronted me, I soon realized that I was looking at Little Alfred.

Did that fit? I fed all the clues and information into Data Control and waited for confirmation. Seconds later, the report flashed across the screen of my mind: "Rhubarb Pie." Apparently we had a small glitch in Data Control's Master Program, so I switched all circuits over to Manual, jacked myself up to a sitting position, and yawned.

That often helps, you know. There's something about a good deep yawn that sweeps all the bird nests out of Data Control's ... whatever-it-is, but the point is that my mind snapped into sharp focus and I found myself staring at Little Alfred.

I shifted over to Questioning Wags on the tail section, as if to say, "What are you doing out here? I thought you were in jail."

His eyes were sparkling. Somehow that worried me. "Hi, Hankie. My time's up and I'm fwee."

Oh. That was nice. And what about the, uh, fishing stuff?

"Mom's taking a nap, so I'd better not wake her up. She needs the west."

Yes, yes? Where was this leading?

The boy rolled his eyes towards the sky. "If she doesn't say no, it means yes."

Wait a minute. That didn't sound exactly right.

"I don't think she'd care if we went down to the cweek, 'cause I'll have my doggie wiff me."

Hmm, good point. I hadn't thought of it that way, but with the Head of Ranch Security in charge of things . . .

"We won't stay wong, and maybe we'll get back before she wakes up. And we can pway Tom Sawyer and Huck Finn. That'll be fun."

Yes, it did sound kind of interesting, a whole lot better than broiling in the afternoon sun and gnawing at fleas, and . . . sure, what the heck.

The boy tiptoed out the gate and closed it without a sound. Then we headed south in a brisk walk, off to see new sights and experience new adventures.

We had an adventure, all right. A bad one.

We Play
Tom Sawyer

As we marched down the hill and past the gas tanks, guess who came out to join us. Drover. I studied him out of the corner of my eye. He was grinning and prancing along and wiggling that stub tail of his and looking very chirpy about things.

"Well, what brings you out of bed so early? It's only three o'clock in the afternoon."

"Oh, there was a hard spot on my gunnysack and I couldn't sleep."

"It wasn't bothering you this morning at four-thirty when I left to go help Slim pull a calf. You seemed to be sleeping very well, but you always do when there's work to do."

"Thanks. Yeah, I love to sleep, and it helps my allergies."

"What allergies?"

"Oh, I've got terrible allergies, and they sure drag me down. I need lots of sleep."

"You don't sound stopped up to me."

He grinned. "Yeah, when I get plenty of rest, they don't bother me, so I guess it works."

"Drover, if you don't show any symptoms, then maybe you don't have allergies. Had you thought about that?"

"Doe, 'cause every wudce id a wile, by dose gets stobbed up ed I ket breathe. See? It just hid be. Baby I deed bore sleeb."

"Drover, I have a feeling that you're allergic to work and Life's harsh realities."

"I sure get stobbed up, I doe that." Just then, he lifted his nose and sniffed the air. "What's that I smell?"

"It's probably your own rotten attitude." I tested the air myself. "I don't smell anything in particular. You must be hearing things."

He sniffed again, and I noticed that his ears perked up. "No, I smell something, and I think it's . . . meat, fresh meat."

I lifted my nose and conducted a more thorough test of the atmosphere and so forth,

and . . . hmm, by George, there was an interesting smell hanging in the air. And yes, it did bear a faint resemblance to the fragrance of . . .

"Drover, I don't want to alarm you, but I'm picking up the smell of fresh meat."

"Oh, that doesn't alarm me, 'cause I smelled it first."

I shot him a piercing glare. "Who's in charge around here, me or you?"

"Well, let's see."

"And which of us has a severe allergenic condition—and therefore can't smell?"

"Oops. Well, by does sure is stobbed up."

"And therefore it follows from simple logic that you couldn't possibly have gotten First Whiff of the Mysterious Fresh Meat. Hencely, and following the same path of simple logic, we arrive at the only possible conclusion, that when I locate this stash of fresh meat, I will get First Dibs."

"Oh drat."

"And we don't need any of your naughty language."

"Oh fiddle."

"That's better. Now, let's see if I can get a fix on this . . . my, my, that's an exciting aroma, isn't it?"

"I ket sbell a thig."

I switched all instruments over to our Locater Program, and within seconds all the data were pointing to a white package which Little Alfred appeared to be carrying . . . hmm, on top of his tackle box. I, uh, tossed a glance at the boy and saw that he wasn't watching, so I quickened my pace just a bit and suddenly found my nose right next to the . . .

WOW!

I turned to Drover. "Holy smokes, Drover, do you realize what we've been smelling?"

"Well, let's see. Fresh liver?"

I narrowed my eyes at him. "I thought you couldn't smell. If you can't smell, what made you think it was fresh liver?"

"I didn't say fresh liver. I said fish lever, and doe, I ket sbell a thig."

"Hmmm, I wonder . . . but never mind. The impointant point is that Little Alfred smuggled a package of fresh liver out of his mother's kitchen, and no doubt he brought it for us. Or to frame it up from another direction, he brought it for ME."

"I just wish I could sbell."

I turned away from Drover and his hypocardiac complaints, and directed my full attention to the package of fresh liver. It was all coming clear now. No doubt the boy realized that he had eaten a "good nourishing lunch" (his mother's very words, right?) and that everyone else on the ranch had eaten a "good nourishing lunch," but that his faithful dog, his dearest friend who had waited for him outside the prison walls—that same dear and faithful friend had not eaten *in days.*

Well, in hours maybe, but it had seemed much longer than that—days and days, weeks and weeks of slow hunger and starvation. Ribs showing. Backbone protruding. Constant dreams about food and rhubarb pie and . . . fresh liver.

Have we ever talked about fresh liver? Wonderful stuff, I love it. Give me a choice between fresh liver and fresh T-bone steak and I'll take the liver every time, especially on fishing trips when, heh-heh, steak isn't on the menu.

No contest at all. "Give me liver or give me death!" I don't remember who said that, but he was a famous American, and he sure knew his liver.

It has a dark red color, liver does, and a dark red taste, and you don't even have to chew it. Just bite off a hunk and let 'er slide down the old guzzle. Great stuff, and I was so touched and happy that my little pal had brought me . . .

Maybe he'd been planning a little picnic down by the creek, but I saw no reason to postpone the instant graffication of . . . that is, once we reached the creek, we'd be busy catching fish and so forth, much too busy to stop for a picnic, so in the interest of time . . .

I, uh, eased my nose over the edge of the tackle box and managed to snag the package with that long tooth on the upper righthand side of my mouth. Then, very carefully I tugged and pulled it into the embrace of my full set of teeth, until I had it in the grisp of my grasp, and then I . . . uh . . . dropped out of the marching formation, shall we say, and let Little Alfred go on without me.

I unslackened my jaws and let the package fall to the ground. There it was! It was mine, all mine, and now all I had to do was remove the papers and . . .

WHACK!

Huh?

Some strange outside force had just struck me on the hinalary region. I uttered a squeak and leaped high into the air and landed several feet away. Once back on earth, I whirled around and . . .

Okay, relax. It was Little Alfred. He had discovered my . . . uh . . . my plan for the Pre-picnic Picnic, and maybe that hadn't pleased him . . . or something. Anyways, he had whacked me across the tail section with his fishing pole, and now he was shaking a finger in my general direction.

"No, no, Hankie. Don't eat my bait."

Oh. Bait. Well, I had never dreamed . . . if he'd only said that it was bait . . . sure, no problem. Yes sir, if that was bait, we sure didn't need to be . . . uh . . . snacking on it, you might say. One of the first rules of fishing is "Never eat your bait." Right?

No problem, no big deal. We'd just had a little mixup in, uh, communications.

The boy placed our package of liver bait back on his tackle box and we resumed our march. I found myself marching next to Drover. I noticed that he was staring at me.

"Yes? You have something to say?"

"Oh, not really. I just wondered what that was all about."

"It was all about bait, Drover. You might have warned me that the purpose of the liver was *bait*."

"Gosh, I never dreamed that liver had a purpose."

"It does, but the question that faces us now is, Do *you* have a purpose?"

"Well, I never thought about that."

"You should think about it. You should think about it long and hard. How does it make you feel that a lowly package of liver has a purpose in this life, and you don't?" He didn't answer. "Hello?"

"Oh, hi. Where do you reckon we're going?"

"We're going fishing, Drover."

"Oh good, how fun. I guess that's why Little Alfred brought his fishing pole and some bait— 'cause we're all going fishing."

I held the runt in the sideward sweep of my eyes for several seconds as I tried to think of an appropriate response. Nothing came to mind, so I just let it drop. That was fine with me. Talking to Drover never leads anywhere. Sometimes I think . . .

Never mind.

CHAPTER NINE

A Bait Thief
Eats Our Liver

By that time we had reached the banks of Wolf Creek. Little Alfred set down his equipment, then he told us dogs to sit down whilst he stood in front of us and gave us our instructions.

"Okay, y'all dogs, we're gonna pway Tom Sawyer. I'll be Tom Sawyer and Hank can be Huck Finn, and Dwover can be . . . who can Dwover be?"

He was looking at me when he asked this. I whapped my tail on the ground and gave him a blank stare, as if to say, "Hey, pal, you're the one who read the book. This is all new to me."

The boy chewed his lip and gave it some heavy thought. "Do you weckon he could be Becky Thatchoo?"

Becky Thatcher? A girl? That didn't sound

80

right to me. Drover was too ugly to be a girl, and besides, he had a stub tail. No girl in a book would ever have a stub tail. I tried to express these thoughts through wags and facial expressions.

Alfred shook his head. "Nah, better not wet him be Becky. We'll pwetend he's Tom's dog, and his name's Dwovoo. How does that sound?"

Drover wasn't listening, so I gave him an elbow in the ribs. "Hey, wake up, you've just been given your assignment."

His eyes came into focus. "Oh, hi. Were you talking to me?"

"We were both talking to you. Do you want to be part of this deal or not?"

"Oh sure, what are we doing?"

"We're playing Tom Sawyer. Alfred is Tom, I'm Huck Finn, and you are Tom's dog."

"Oh good. That sure fits, 'cause I'm a dog. What's my name?"

"Your name is Drover."

He grinned. "I'll be derned. That's my name too. This'll be easy." His grin faded. "Now, let's see. I'm Drover and you're Hank Finn, so who's Alfred?"

"Alfred is Tom Sawyer."

"Oh. Who's Tom Sawyer?"

"Alfred. I just said that."

"Yeah, but I mean really."

"He's ... I don't know who he is. Some guy in a book."

"What if we haven't read the book?"

I glared at the runt. "Do you want to play or not? It's all pretend, it's not meant to be Reality as It Really Is. If it's too complicated, then maybe you ought to run along."

There was a moment of silence. "You mean, my name really isn't Drover?"

"No, your name really IS Drover, but we're also pretending that it's Drover."

"If my name really is Drover, how come we have to pretend?"

Many thoughts marched across the parade ground of my mind as I looked into the emptiness of his eyes. "Drover, please shut up."

"Sure, I can handle that. I just ... "

"Hush!"

Whew! I turned away from him and tried to shake the vapors out of my head. That little mutt could take a simple idea and run it straight into the ground.

Well, whilst I had been listening to Drover's blabber, Little Alfred had opened up the package of ... mmmmmm ... the package of liver, so to speak, and had baited his hook with a hunk

of . . . boy, that stuff smelled wonderful, but of course I now realized that it was merely bait.

Fishing bait. Bait for the fish. It was strictly off-limits to us dogs.

The boy pitched his line out into the water. "Okay, dogs, here comes a big old fish."

The line plunked into the water and the cork bobbed to the surface. We sat down on the bank and waited. And waited. And waited. I found myself stealing glances at Alfred. Where was the fish? I didn't mean to complain, but if a guy's going to fish, he ought to catch one, right?

We were just . . . *staring at the cork*. I mean, it was a great little cork, white with red stripes, but show me a great little cork and I'll show you something I don't need to stare at for very long.

I found myself getting restless. I moved my front paws up and down. I whimpered. When that didn't tear Alfred's attention away from the cork, I decided to try something bolder. I barked.

His eyes came up. "Shhhh. You'll scare the fish."

Oops. Sorry. But if you asked me . . .

Hmmm. All at once it dawned on me that the boy was very muchly preoccupied with his, uh, fishing experience, which meant . . .

Which meant that I needed to, uh, stretch my legs and, you know, walk around a little bit to . . . well, stretch my legs and muscles and bodily fluids. It's not good for a dog to sit in one spot for too long, don't you know, because . . . well, it just isn't good.

So I eased myself to a standing position and entered into a Yawn and Stretch Procedure. The boy wasn't watching, so I took several steps to the north, which more or less placed me out of his line of sight. I paused to see if he would notice or call me back. He did neither.

Okay, I had just been cleared to take a little . . . uh stroll, a short walk around the immediate area to loosen up my muscles and so forth. By sheer chance and coincidence, my footsteps led me towards . . . by George, it was a piece of white wrapping paper, lying there on the sand and flapping in the breeze.

Now, wasn't that odd? What would a piece of wrapping paper be doing down here beside the creek? Perhaps some careless person had tossed it out the window of a passing . . . well, car or pickup or maybe even an airplane. Yes, that was it, an airplane. Some careless person or persons had thrown garbage out the window of a passing airplane, and you know where I stand on the issue of garbage and litter.

I don't allow it, not on my outfit.

And so it was perfectly natural that I took one last glance at Little Alfred (he wasn't watching) and decided that I sure needed to, uh, check out this shocking case of littering. I altered my course and headed straight for the . . .

HUH?

The liver was gone!

I froze. My mind tumbled. At last the pieces of

the puzzle began falling into place. We had a Bait Thief running loose on the ranch. Whilst we'd been preoccupied with the Fishing Experience, some cheating sneaking thieving outlaw rascal had sneaked into our camp and stolen all of Little Alfred's bait!

I was furious. What kind of brute would steal bait from a five-year-old boy? What was this world coming to? I mean, if an innocent child can't go fishing on his own family's ranch without getting his bait stolen . . .

I gave the empty paper a good sniffing, just to make sure . . . WOW! . . . just to make sure I wasn't barking up a blind tree, and I wasn't. The strong aroma of . . . well, bait, still lingered on the empty paper.

Okay, somebody would pay for this. I made a vow then and there not to rest or sleep until I had brought this thief to justice.

I rushed over to the spot where Drover was sitting and looking up at the clouds. I dropped my voice to a low murmur. "Drover, I don't want to alarm you, but I'm afraid we've got a Bait Thief running loose on the ranch."

His eyes drifted down from the clouds. "Oh, hi. What's a Bait Thief?"

"It's someone or something who steals bait,

such as an entire package of raw liver."

"I'll be derned. You mean Little Alfred's liver?"

"Not his own liver, but the package of beef liver he brought along as bait. It's all gone. Someone stole it."

"I'll be derned."

"You don't seem alarmed."

He grinned. "Well, you told me not to be alarmed, so I guess I'm not."

"Hmmm, yes. Nice work."

"Thanks."

I studied him more closely. "Drover, you've got something red on your lips. When you're on duty, I'd appreciate it if you'd show a little more pride in your personal appearance. After all, we are the elite forces of the Security Division."

"Sorry." He licked his lips. "There, is that better?"

"Much better. Thanks. I don't want to be a nag, but we do have an image to protect. Now, I need to ask you a few questions."

"Oh good. I was getting kind of bored."

"Right. Fishing is for the birds."

"Yeah, and there's several right up there."

"Several what?"

He looked up to the sky. I followed his gaze and sure enough . . . "Oh yes, birds. Actually, they are hawks, Drover, a variety of raptor bird we have on this ranch."

"No, I think they're buzzards."

I squinted my eyes and took a closer look. "Okay, maybe they're buzzards. At first glance, the two resemble one another, but your buzzards are bigger and darker than your hawks."

"Maybe they ate the liver."

I stared at him for a long moment. "What?"

"I said, maybe those buzzards ate the liver. That's what they do. They fly around and look for something to eat."

My gaze lingered on him for several seconds, then I turned and paced several steps away from him. "Drover, there's something here that troubles me."

"Yeah, I know. They shouldn't have stolen Alfred's bait."

"No, it's even more troubling than that." I paced back over to him. "Something very strange is going on here. You see, what you just said about the buzzards makes a certain amount of sense."

"What's wrong with that?"

"Nothing's wrong with it. Making sense is good, it's important, it's something we try to do in the Security Business." I stopped pacing and whirled around. "But Drover, it's not something *you* do very often, which makes me just a little bit suspicious."

"I'll be derned." Just then he burped. "Oops, sorry. I guess I ate too fast."

"No problem. It happens even to the best of us. Now, back to what I was . . ." I froze. "Wait a minute. What do you mean, *you ate too fast*?"

"Well, I guess I should have chewed up my food a little better, instead of gulping it down. When I gulp, I get indigestion. It happens every time."

I narrowed my eyes and studied his face. My mind was racing by this time, and I found myself sifting clues that were leading this case in an entirely new direction. Here, check this out.

Clue #1: A package of fresh liver suddenly and mysteriously disappeared.

Clue #2: Drover had something red on his lips, remember?

Clue #3: Out of nowhere, Drover came up with a fairly reasonable explanation for the disappearance of the liver. (The buzzards.)

Clue #4: Drover belched.

Clue #5: Upon belching, he said something about "eating too fast."

Do you see how all these pieces began to fit together? All at once I had a prime suspect in the case, and it sure as thunder wasn't a buzzard.

I should have known. How could I have been such a blockhead? I was too nice, that was it, too trusting of my friend and fellow-dog, for you see . . .

Hang on. This might come as a terrible shock.

. . . for you see, I now had enough evidence to wrap this case up, and the evidence pointed like a flaming arrow . . . *at Drover.*

I marched over to him and stuck my nose in his face. "Drover, I hate to tell you this, but there's something fishy going on around here."

Drover leaped to his feet. "Yeah, Little Alfred just caught one, and I guess we'd better go help him."

Huh?

Sure enough, the boy had just pulled in a big catfish.

CHAPTER TEN

Disaster Strikes

All at once, it was All Hands on Deck. People and dogs and catfish were running in all directions. Well, the people and dogs were running, but the fish was . . .

Let's slow down, take a deep breath, and try to get all this sorted out. It was kind of confusing, to tell you the truth, because so much was going on at once.

First off, my interrogation of Drover came to a sudden stop, which was rotten luck because I had reached the Critical Phase and had been on the point of springing my trap on the little cheat and charging him with Liver Theft, a very serious crime on our ranch.

But you see, at that very moment Little Alfred's

cork disappeared and he pulled in a big flapping catfish. To add even more drama to the drama, the flapping fish somehow flapped the hook out of his mouth. This occurred in midair and the fish fell to the ground.

The boy let out a whoop of joy. Then, when he saw the fish hit the ground, he threw down his pole and started yelling at us.

"Come on, doggies, and help me catch my fish before he jumps back in the cweek!"

Well, you know how I am about these kids. When they put out a Distress Call, I drop everything and go straight into a Code Three situation. Drover and I arrived on the scene at approximately the same time. The fish was flopping around and edging closer to the water.

I turned to Drover. "Well, don't just stand there. Do something."

"Well . . . I don't know what to do."

"Jump in and grab the fish, what do you think?"

"Yeah, but he's all slimy and yucky, and what if he slaps me with his tail?"

I pushed him aside. "Drover, you're worthless. Oh, and by the way, I know who ate that package of liver."

"Yeah, it was those darned old buzzards."

"Not buzzards, Drover."

"You'd better grab the fish."

"Don't tell me what to do. Get out of my way. I'll deal with you later. Watch this and study your lessons."

I swaggered into the situation and sized it up with one quick sweep of the eyes. It was a timing deal, see. You wait until the fish has quit flapping, then you charge in and grab him. I waited for just the right moment, then darted in and . . .

BLAP!

. . . the stupid fish landed a lucky punch with his tail, right on the end of my nose. No problem, no big deal. I went into a crouch, studied the pattern of the rhythm of his . . . whatever . . . his flopping maneuver, I guess you'd call it, and then I launched a second . . .

BLAP!

. . . and this time the stupid fish not only slapped me, but also stuck a fin into the soft leathery portion of my nose. Did it hurt? You bet it did. Have we discussed catfish fins? They are long and sharp and very dangerous, and getting stuck by a catfish fin is no cup of worms.

I uttered a yelp of pain and backed out of the struggle. My nose throbbed and my eyes

had begun to water. I turned my watering eyes towards the runt.

"Drover, if you don't do something, the fish is going to get away."

"Okay, here we go. I'll bark at him."

And he did, if that's what you want to call yipping and squeaking. I would have been ashamed to call it "barking." He yipped and squeaked— and to no one's surprise, kept a safe distance between himself and the fish.

Little Alfred was getting worried. "Come on, Hankie, gwab my fish! I want to take him home and show my mom."

I heaved a sigh. Okay, it was down to me . . . up to me . . . the entire responsibility for the mission had fallen upon my shoulders, let us say, and I had no choice but to wade back into combat— and never mind all the slaps on the face, all the barbs in the nose.

I waited for just the right moment, then launched myself high in the . . .

SPLASH!

He got away. The idiot fish got away! All three of us stood there on the bank and watched him swim away. Little Alfred flopped down in the sand and plunged into a Deep Pout, and we're talking about tragic eyes and pooched lips.

I whirled around to Drover. "Now look what you've done. You've let the fish get away and now our little pal has a broken heart. I hope you're happy. Oh, and by the way, Drover, we have linked you to the stolen liver."

"I thought the buzzards did it."

"No. It was you. We know it was you. You know it was you. How could you have committed such a selfish act of selfishness?"

His lip curled down and a tear slipped out of the corner of one eye. "Well . . . I was hungry, and I was afraid you'd eat it all."

"Me? You actually thought I would steal bait from my little pal? Ha! What a wild and corrupt imagination you have. I'm shocked, Drover, shocked and outraged and very, very disappointed in you."

"Well . . ." He was crying now. "It smelled so good and I was starving and I just couldn't resist."

"There! Now we've come to the core of the root. You couldn't resist. Son, those of us in the Security Business are trained to resist all temptation. We are sworn to resist. We are bound by our Cowdog Oath to resist."

"I know, I'm a thief, I'm a failure, I'm a disgrace to the ranch."

"Yes, you are. It's true. In a moment of weakness, you yielded to temptation. What you didn't realize..."

Hmmm. At that very moment, and I mean right in the middle of this important lecture, my eyes fell upon a scrap of liver lying on the ground, right at my very feet. I darted my nose down to it, sniffed it, and gulped it down.

"What you failed to realize was that you left one scrap of liver for me, you greedy little goat, and now..."

HUH?

There was a cork hanging in the air, right in front of my chin, a white cork with a red stripe down the middle. Hadn't I seen that cork before, or one just like it? And how could a cork just... hang in front of a guy's...

I shot a glance at Drover. His eyes were wide and his mouth hung open. I shot a glance at Alfred. He was staring at me too, and the expression on his face showed... well, shock. Fear. Astonishment. There was a long, throbbing moment of silence. Then...

Little Alfred spoke. "Oh my. Hankie, you just swallowed my fishhook!"

I did? Swallowed a fishhook? But I'd thought... see, there was this piece of liver just lying there on the bank and...

Oh for Pete's sakes, *that had been his bait*! He'd caught the fish with that very hook and bait, only the stupid fish hadn't swallowed it and it had popped out of his . . .

Gulp.

The three of us exchanged Looks of Greatest Concern. I switched my tail over to Slow Mournful Wags.

The boy's face had turned pale. "What are we gonna do now?"

I . . . I didn't have an answer to that, but something told me that it wasn't good for a dog to have a fishhook in his stomach. See, as long as the liver stayed on the hook, the barb, the deadly barb, was covered up. But guess what happens to liver in a dog's stomach. It gets digested, and then . . .

Gulp.

We had a serious problem here, and the way I framed it up, we had maybe an hour to get that hook out of my innards, before . . .

Drover fell apart and started moaning. Little Alfred began to cry. "I wish we hadn't come fishing. My doggie ate a fishhook and . . . I want my mommy!"

So they both moaned and cried, and what was I supposed to do? I just sat there, staring at that silly cork. At last the boy got control of himself.

"We bettoo go home, fast. I'll cut the stwing."

I wasn't so sure that was a good idea, but I wasn't so sure it was a bad one either. I mean, what were you supposed to do in this situation? If you tried to pull the string, it might cause the hook to dig into . . . but if you cut the string and left it there . . .

Yikes.

Alfred found a pocket knife in his tackle box and cut the string. I hardly knew how to respond when I felt the string slipping down into my . . . yes, we sure needed to make a fast trip back to the house.

Alfred and I ran. Drover limped along behind. I could hear him moaning. "Oh, it's all my fault and I feel so guilty, and this leg's about to kill me, oh my leg!"

That helped a bunch, all his moaning and groaning and feeling guilty.

At last we reached headquarters and went streaking into the yard. Sally May was outside, working in her flower beds again, and Baby Molly was lying on a blanket nearby. When Sally May heard us coming, she straightened up and stared at us for a moment. Somehow she knew that we were bringing trouble.

Didn't I tell you? She reads minds.

She dropped her trowel and met us at the gate. "What's wrong, Alfred? Are you all right? What's happened?" The boy started crying and blurted out the whole story. When Sally May heard the part about the swallowed fishhook, her eyes seemed to . . . well, roll back into her head. "I knew it. Alfred, honey, that's why Mommy didn't want you to go fishing without an adult."

"Mom, what can we do to save Hankie?"

She thought for a moment, her eyes flicking back and forth from me to Alfred. "I don't know. Run get your dad. No, wait. He's in the alfalfa field. Run get Slim. He's welding in the machine shed. Maybe he'll know what to do."

Alfred took off running for the machine shed. When he was gone, I found myself . . . well, all alone with . . . uh . . . Sally May, and I must admit that it made me very uncomfortable. I mean, just that very morning we had sort of patched things up and started over with our, uh, relationship, and now . . . this.

I could tell, just by looking at her, that she wasn't real happy about this. For a long time she stared down at me, shaking her head and moving her lips. Then . . . you won't believe this . . . then she knelt down, took my face in her hands, and sang a song. Here's how it went.

CHAPTER ELEVEN

A Deadly Hook Lurks in My Stomach

Sally May's Lament

Hank, I just don't understand,
What's your plan, how you can
Do the crazy things that you do.
I can make no sense at all,
Off the wall, of all the gall,
Tell me this is not really true.

How in thunderation, Hank, could you have
     done this latest thing?
Swallowed down a fishhook—and even ate
     the string!

I don't want to get involved,
Don't ask me to try to solve
This latest brainless stunt that you've
    hatched.
I have many things to do,
Not including things that you
Bring to me and drop in my lap.

I deserve my quiet time, planting flowers
   in my yard.
But here you are again—good Lord, you make
   it hard!

How's a woman to react
To this latest stupid act?
Don't we give you plenty to eat?
If we took the money that
We spend on dogs, spend on cats,
We could buy a mountain retreat.

We've tried to raise our son up right, filled his
   room with noble books.
But his best friend is a dog—who gobbles
   fishing hooks!

By the time she had finished her song, I heard
footsteps behind me. I turned and saw Slim and
Alfred coming into the yard. Alfred was tugging
at Slim's hand, trying to get some speed out of
him, but that wasn't easy. Slim does things at
his own pace, which is somewhere between slow
and slower.

But at last they arrived on the scene. Sally
May cast a worried glance towards Slim. So did
Little Alfred. So did I. I mean, this was a time to

be worried, right? He pushed his hat to the back of his head and shifted his toothpick to the other side of his mouth.

"Ate a fishhook, huh?"

Well, I . . . no, I didn't exactly eat a fishhook. That would have been a silly thing to do. I ate a piece of meat, see, and it happened to be attached to a . . . well, to a hook. A fishhook. So to answer the question, yes, a fishhook had been swallowed.

Slim shook his head. "Hank, you are such a birdbrain."

I . . . I didn't know how to respond to that, so I swept my tail across the grass and tried to squeeze up a little smile.

Sally May spoke. "Slim, is there anything . . . look, I don't want to sound cruel and unfeeling, but our budget this month is tight. There's nothing in it for major surgery at the vet clinic to remove a . . ." She shot me a glare. ". . . a fishhook from a dog's stomach, for crying out loud."

"Uh-huh."

"So is there something we might try . . . is there anything we could do here to get it out? I'll be honest, Slim, this is beyond the realm of my experience."

"Yalp." He shifted his weight to his other leg. "Well, there might be. I went through this once before with a dog that ate a turkey heart that was attached to a hook."

"Yes, and?"

"You've got to make the dog throw it up. Soap. You got some dish warshing soap in a squeeze bottle?"

"Yes, right beside the sink. Alfred, go fetch it, and hurry."

The boy headed for the house in a run. Slim continued. "See, you squirt the soap into his mouth and hold his jaws shut, so's he can't spit it out. Once he swallers enough of it, his old stomach'll pitch it back up."

"How dainty."

"And if you're lucky, the hook'll come out with the soap."

"I see. And if it doesn't?"

He shrugged. "If his stomach dissolves that piece of liver, it'll expose the barb, and then we might have a problem."

Sally May looked off to the horizon. "The things we do for our children."

"Yalp. But maybe it'll work."

Alfred came flying out of the house and handed Slim a white plastic squeeze bottle. Then the boy hugged his momma's leg and watched. Slim took a deep breath and sat down in the grass. He dragged me over to him and threw a leg around my middle.

"Are you ready for this, pooch? It ain't going to be fun for either one of us, but even less for you than for me. Open up."

Okay, I was as ready for it as I ever would be. It was just soap, right? A squirt or two of soap and then it would all be over. I figured I could handle it. What was a little dab of soap in the mouth? No big deal, and a whole lot better than a fishhook. Yes, I was ready.

I heard the wheeze of the squeeze bottle, and felt something soft and warm upon my tongualary region. This wasn't so . . . but he kept shooting that stuff into my mouth, and all at once . . . hey, that was enough . . . all at once my mouth began picking up the taste of . . .

THAT STUFF TASTED HORRIBLE!

Hey, forget this. I thought we'd been talking about a little dab of soap, but he just kept pumping it in there! I began flicking my tongue back and forth, in a desperate effort to get that nasty stuff out of my mouth, but you know what he did? *He clamped my jaws shut and held on!*

I couldn't spit. My mouth was filling up with . . . with slimy soap and bubbles and yucky foam, and all at once I was having trouble breathing and . . . okay, I had to swallow it, just to get it

out of my mouth so I could breathe!

I swallowed. It was awful, but at least the deed was done.

Slim patted me on the head. "Way to go, pooch, we're done with Step One. Three more treatments and maybe we'll get some results."

I stared at him in disbelief. What? Three more treatments, my foot! No way, Charlie. If I had to die, let it be from a fishhook, not from Soap Poisoning.

Just for a second he relaxed his leg-lock around my middle. I saw my opportunity and went into Digging Mode on all four legs. I fought and struggled with all my might, and all at once I popped out of his grasp. Once free, I set sail for the front yard.

Behind me, I could hear Slim yelling. "Hank, come here, boy. Here Hankie, nice doggie, come on back."

Ha! Was he crazy? No thanks. I'd swallowed all the soap I needed for about fifty years.

"Alfred, go around the north side of the house. We've got to catch him and get some more soap down him. If you get close, jump him and hang on. I'll go around the south side of the house."

I heard them coming. I dived underneath a cedar bush in front of the house and peered out. I could see them now—Alfred creeping around the northeast corner of the house and Slim coming around the southeast corner. Sally May followed Slim, with Baby Molly riding on her hip.

They all met near the yard gate. They were looking around in all directions and talking in low voices. They couldn't see me. I was safe, as long as . . .

HARK!

What lousy luck. One of those soap bubbles got caught in my throat, and it was either cough or choke. I coughed and they heard it. All three pairs of eyes pointed straight at me, and Slim began creeping towards the shrub.

"Come on, Hankie, we've got to get that hook out of you before it's too late. Come on, boy, be a nice puppy."

Ha! I'd heard that before, that "nice puppy" business, and it had always meant bad news for me. No way. If they wanted to sit around and eat soap all afternoon, that was fine, but they'd do it without me.

I lay there, motionless, and watched as Slim dropped down on his hands and knees. "Come on, Hankie, just a little more."

No. I wasn't coming out, never ever.

Then Little Alfred came up. His lip was trembling and he had tears shining in his eyes. "Hankie, come out, pweese. I don't want you to die fwom a hook. Eat some more soap, pweese."

Well...how can a dog say no to his fishing buddy, his best pal in the world? If Alfred thought I needed some more soap...ugh...

I lay still while Slim reached his hand into my hiding place. He caught me by a back leg and pulled me out.

He leg-locked me again and we continued with the Soapotherapy. Did it work? Was I saved from the Deadly Fishhook?

I'm sorry, I can't reveal that information. It's too scary, too secret and sensitive. If you want to find out, you'll have to keep on reading.

CHAPTER TWELVE

Major Surgery, a Deathbed Vigil, and . . .

Whilst Slim held me in a leg-lock, Sally May held my front paws and stroked me on the head. And you know what? Looking up into her eyes, I could see that she was really worried about me. I was touched and surprised.

I mean, we'd been through some hard times, Sally May and I. We'd seen bad days when I had been pretty sure she didn't like me, and . . . well, I must admit that on a few occasions I had experienced a few, uh, raw feelings about her too.

Might as well go ahead and blurt it out. There had been moments in our relationship when I'd thought she was mean, gripey, and totally unreasonable. There, I said it. But you know what? As I lay there in the grass with my head in her lap, looking up into her eyes and feeling the soft touch of her hand, all those bad feelings just . . . vanished.

All at once we were friends. It was kind of touching, and it helped take my mind off of the Soapotherapy. How bad was it? Think of the worst-tasting gunk you can imagine, then multiply it by ten. It was bad, real bad.

Slim continued squirting the awful stuff into my mouth and forcing me to swallow it. I was drowning in soap bubbles, but I didn't try to run away. They were doing their best to save me, and the least I could do was . . . well, stick around and be saved.

But the funny thing about the deal was that, even though the soap tasted terrible, it wasn't making me sick. I mean, I knew that's what they wanted, that was the whole purpose of pumping me full of soap, and I was ready and willing to go right into the Upchuck Phase. But you can't upchuck if you don't feel sick, and I didn't feel sick.

At last Slim set down the bottle, removed his hat, and scratched the top of his head. "This ain't working. I've given him half a bottle of soap and he ain't even burped yet. Good honk, that's enough soap to make an elephant sick." He gnawed at his lip. "I've got one more idea."

He pushed himself up off the grass. I heard his knees pop. He slapped his hat back on his head and took a deep breath of air. "I'm gonna spin him around in circles. Maybe when he gets dizzy, it'll make him want to toss his cookies. It always worked for me at the carnival."

Sally May arched her brows. "I wouldn't have thought of that."

"Me neither, but when a guy runs out of luck, he's forced to use his brain. I've always tried to avoid that, but once in a while it's forced upon us. We'll see if it works."

Sally May and Little Alfred watched with big worried eyes. Slim took my front paws in his hands and started spinning me around. And around. And around. On the first few twirls, I felt as though my body might pull in half, but after that initial impression . . .

By George, it was kind of fun. I had never gone swooping and flying around in circles before, or seen the sky spinning around above my head while the wind rushed past my ears. Hey, this was neat! It was even more exciting than riding in the back of a pickup or chasing after the mail truck.

Around and around we went, faster and faster. I could almost imagine that I was flying a jet fighter or riding a spaceship to the moon. Heck of a fun ride, and I was kind of disappointed when I felt Slim slowing down. We slowed to a stop and he turned loose of my legs.

I stood up and . . . well, I tried to walk but, by George, the old ground seemed to be spinning around. I walked sideways four or five steps and fell down. Yes sir, either the ground was shifting or else something had caused my old legs to turn to rubber. I got up again and staggered around some more.

I heard Alfred laugh. "Wook at Hank, he's so dizzy he can't walk."

Dizzy? Okay, maybe that was it. All that spinning around had made me dizzy, and no doubt I looked pretty funny, staggering around like a drunk spider. But you know what was even funnier? Slim. He'd given me the ride, but he turned out to be even dizzier than I was. And I don't think he'd expected that to happen.

See, once he'd quit spinning me and had set me down, he was just standing there in his normal fashion. Then all at once he was running sideways and fell into Sally May's flower bed. She rushed over and tried to help him up.

"Oh dear, Slim, are you all right?"

"Oh yeah, shore. Just help me up." He got to his feet and staggered sideways again. "You know, I'm beginning to remember how come I quit going to the carnival. All that round and around stuff makes me a little . . ."

All at once he turned west and went staggering around to the backside of the house. A moment later we heard him . . . uh . . . "calling Earl," as they say.

"Earl! Earl!"

Alfred gave his mom a puzzled look. All at once she was fussing with a string on her blouse.

"What's he doing, Mom?"

"Shhh. He's not feeling well."

The boy grinned. "He got sick? But he was twying to make Hankie sick!"

"Alfred, shhh. The less said about this, the better."

Slim returned. His hat sat crooked on his head, his face was pale, and he was walking on stiff legs. He beamed a glare at me and shook his head.

"Sally May, I don't know what it takes to make that dog throw up, but I've about decided that I ain't man enough to do it."

She closed her eyes for a moment. "He has thrown up on my shoe, on my foot, on my kitchen floor, on my living-room carpet, in my yard, on my porch. He has never missed an opportunity to throw up on something clean and nice. But you give him half a bottle of soap and spin him around in circles . . ." She didn't finish the sentence. Her eyes slid open, and she was wearing a crazy smile. "You know, Slim, if this were happening to someone else, it would be hilarious."

"Yes ma'am, it sure might be."

She brushed a wisp of hair on Molly's forehead. "But it's happening to us. Well, I guess you'd better," she heaved a sigh, "take him to town. The poor thing needs a doctor."

"He needs a psychiatrist, is what he needs. You want me to haul him in my pickup? It already stinks. If he barfs, nobody'll know the difference."

"Yes, please."

She walked with us to Slim's old pickup, which was parked in the shade beneath those big elm trees west of the gas tanks. Slim slid behind the wheel, Little Alfred rode shotgun, and I sat in the seat between them. And all at once, I wasn't feeling so swell.

Sally May gave Alfred a kiss on the cheek. "Have a safe trip. Alfred, be kind to Slim and don't chatter all the way to town. He's had a bad day."

Slim nodded and hit the starter. The motor turned over three times . . . and quit. The battery was dead. Silence moved over us like a poisonous fog. No one dared to move or speak. Slim stared at the ignition key for several moments, licked his lips, and turned to Sally May.

"I've been meaning to charge up this derned battery. What do we do now?"

That same crazy smile leaped across her mouth. "Well! I guess you'll haul him to town in my car." She turned a menacing glare on her son. "Alfred, don't you EVER go fishing again. And you . . ." She leaned into the window and turned her glare on . . . well, on ME, it seemed. "If you throw up in my car, I'll murder you! I will, I promise, and with my bare hands."

My goodness, yes ma'am. We sure didn't need that.

We loaded up in her car and set out for town. The silence was deadly. Slim gripped the wheel with both hands and glared at the road with a pair of smoldering eyes. Every now and then he would throw a glance at me and mutter.

"Dumbbell dog ... I can't believe you'd ... hauling you to town when I've got thirty-seven jobs to do ... swallered half a gallon of dadgum soap and ... "

Maybe he didn't know it but I felt terrible about causing everyone so much trouble. A lot of dogs wouldn't have cared. I mean, they just blunder through Life and never think about the people around them, but I have a tender side to my ...

Boy, it seemed kind of warm inside that car.

I have a tender side to my nature that isn't always obvious to the outside world. They see me as Head of Ranch ...

I sure wished he would open a window and let in a breeze.

Anyways, they see me as Head of Ranch Security and they think I'm made of steel and have no feelings about ...

All at once I noticed the swaying motion of the car. Maybe if Slim slowed down a bit ... and I found my thoughts turning to ... SOAP. I began tapping my tail on the floorboard. It was a sort of warning tap. He didn't notice. I turned a Gaze of Urgency towards Little Alfred, but he didn't notice either.

I felt a certain queazy feeling deep in the

internal innards of my ... I increased the speed and urgency of my tail tapping. Somebody needed to open the window and stop flying over cattle-guards, because if somebody didn't do something pretty quick ...

I struggled to my feet. My head was moving up and down, driven by deep mysterious forces that I couldn't ... all at once, the entire world had turned to soap. I could feel it, taste it, smell it, almost hear it. Everywhere and everything, yucky soap!

The convulsions seized my body and took control. I fell into their grip and was helpless. Things were beyond my control ... but just then ...

It was Little Alfred who finally noticed. "Uh-oh. Swim, stop the car!"

The brakes screamed and I went crashing into the dashboard. An instant later, both doors flew open and someone dragged me out of the car by my hind legs. And fellers, you talk about dodging a bullet. We dodged a big one, and not a moment too soon. There, on the side of the Wolf Creek Road, I laid down a long trail of soap bubbles.

I will never feel the same about soap.

Or liver.

The good news is that the hook came up with the soap. Slim saw it right away and held it up for all of us to see. "Well, there she is. By grabs, Hank, you done one thing right today. You saved us a trip to town. Good dog."

Good dog? I stared at him through watering eyes and waves of... something, whatever you call the waves that were rippling through my mind and body... and then I had to return to my business.

Well, we made it back to the ranch about fifteen minutes after we'd left. Sally May heard us coming and ran out to the gate to meet us. She knew something had happened, and her face resembled stone as she waited for the report. When she heard the news, her expression softened and she heaved a big sigh of relief.

Hey, and she even knelt down, placed my head on her knee, and stroked the top of my head, and we're talking about High Quality Stroking here. She stroked my head and scratched me behind the ears, and she even talked to me in a soft tone of voice.

"Poor old Hank. I'll bet that soap was awful. You don't feel very good, do you?"

I felt lousy. I mean, it was nice knowing that I had gotten rid of the fishhook, but all that soap had finally taken its toll. I was one sick puppy.

Sally May's eyes came up and stuck Little

Alfred. "Alfred Leroy, don't you EVER sneak off and go fishing again, do you hear me?"

He nodded. "I'm sowwy, Mom. I'll nevoo do it again, pwomise." He went over and gave her a hug. For a moment she seemed stiff and angry, but then she softened up and drew him into her embrace.

Then she glanced up at Slim and gave her head a shake. "Boys and dogs. I guess life would be pretty dull without them."

"Yalp. Can't say as I ever swung a dog around in circles and got sick before. On this outfit, a guy never knows what sort of work he'll be doing."

They got a laugh out of that. I managed a weak smile. We had reached a happy ending to the story, but I was too full of soap to enjoy it.

And that's about it. I had managed to solve the Case of the Swallowed Fishhook and had lived to tell the story. Two days later, I was back to full strength, protecting my ranch from monsters and taking care of business. The Case of the Swallowed Fishhook had led me right up to Death's Doormat, but the pain and so forth had taught me a valuable lesson. I even composed a song about it, if you can believe that. You want to hear it? I guess we have time. Here it is, and then I've got to get back to work.

I Will Never Eat Another Fishhook

I have learned a lot from this experience.
I feel older and even wiser from the pain.
There's a lesson here for those who pay
    attention.
Life can teach us if we'll only use our brain.
Learn from pain.
Use our brain.

We should try to avoid ingesting fishhooks.
Yes, I know it's the liver that we crave,
But it's wrapped around a barb of sharpened
    metal
That can lead unwary dogs into the grave.
Things we crave.
Early grave.

See, a dog can't go around just eating
    garbage.
We must learn to eat the things that make us
    strong.
Certain foods, like sharpened hooks, have
    poor nutrition.
And that road into the vet's is very long.
Make us strong.
Road is long.

I will never eat another fishhook.
I take a pledge, I swear an oath, I have a
    plan.
And the next time I confront some tasty
    morsel . . .
I'll probably eat it and go through this all
    again.
Not much plan.
All again.

See you down the road. Case closed.

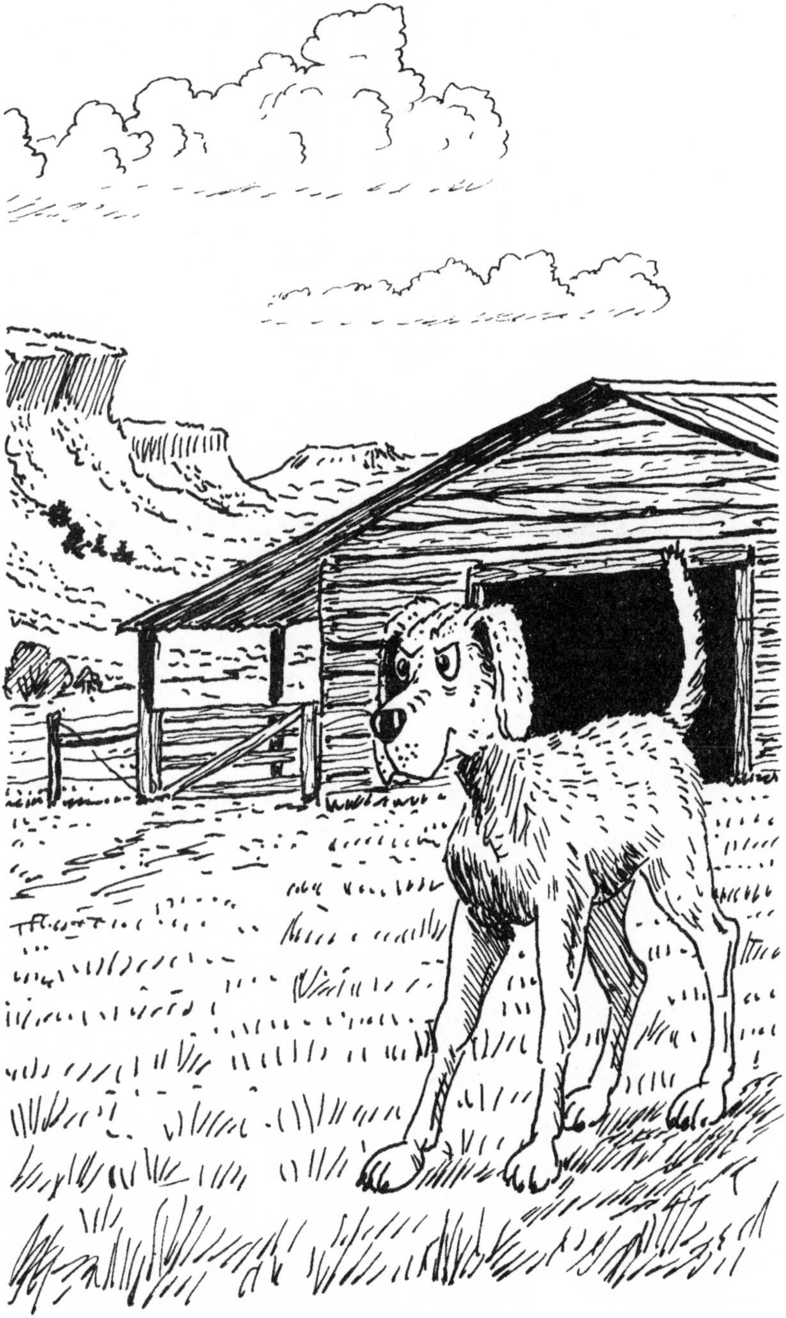

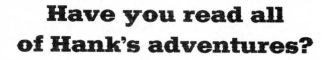

Have you read all of Hank's adventures?

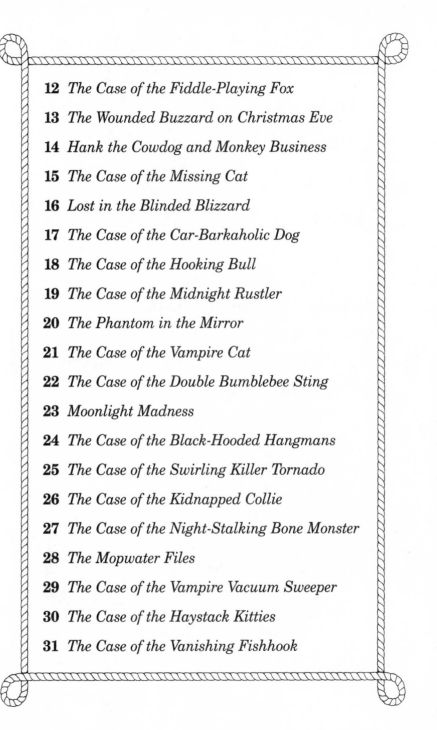

Join Hank the Cowdog's Security Force

Are you a big Hank the Cowdog fan? Then you'll want to join Hank's Security Force. Here is some of the neat stuff you will receive:

Welcome Package
- A Hank paperback embossed with Hank's top secret seal
- Free Hank bookmarks

Eight issues of *The Hank Times* with
- Stories about Hank and his friends
- Lots of great games and puzzles
- Special previews of future books
- Fun contests

More Security Force Benefits

- Special discounts on Hank books and audiotapes
- An original Hank poster (19" x 25") absolutely free

For more information write to:

Hank's Security Force
Maverick Books
PO Box 549
Perryton, Texas 79070

John R. Erickson

began writing stories in 1967 while working full-time as a cowboy, farmhand, and ranch manager in Texas and Oklahoma—where two of the dogs were Hank and his sidekick Drover. Hank the Cowdog made his debut a long time ago in the pages of *The Cattleman*, a magazine about cattle for adults. Soon after, Erickson began receiving "Dear Hank" letters and realized that many of his eager fans were children.

The Hank the Cowdog series won Erickson a *Publishers Weekly* "Listen Up" Award for Best Humor in Audio. He also received an Audie from the Audio Publishers Association for Outstanding Children's Series.

The author of more than thirty-five books, Erickson lives with his wife, Kris, and their three children on a ranch near his boyhood home of Perryton, Texas.